How the Rake Tempted the Lady

How the Rake Tempted the Lady

Laura A. Barnes

Laura A. Barnes

2021

First Printing: 2021

ISBN: 9798738578168

Laura A. Barnes

Website: www.lauraabarnes.com

Cover Art by Cheeky Covers

Editor: Telltail Editing

To: Everyone who believes in the magic of love at first sight.

Cast of Characters

Hero ~ Barrett Ralston

Heroine ~ Gemma Holbrooke

Uncle Theo ~ Duke of Colebourne

Lucas Gray ~ Colebourne's son

Susanna Forrester ~ Colebourne's sister-in-law

Duncan Forrester ~ Lady Forrester's son/Colebourne's nephew

Jacqueline Holbrooke ~ Colebourne's niece

Charlotte Holbrooke ~ Colebourne's niece

Jasper Sinclair ~ Charlotte's husband

Evelyn Holbrooke ~ Colebourne's niece

Reese Worthington ~ Evelyn's husband

Graham (Worth) Worthington ~ Reese Worthington's brother

Noel Worthington ~ Reese Worthington's sister

Abigail Cason ~ Colebourne's ward

Selina Pemberton ~ Lucas Gray's fiancée

Duke of Norbury ~ Selina Pemberton's father

Duke & Duchess of Theron – Barrett Ralston's parents

Barbara Langdale ~ Reese Worthington's ex-mistress

Prologue

Lucas Gray stormed inside his father's study after Lord Ralston left. Lady Forrester, his Aunt Susanna, followed on his heels. While Ralston held his appointment with his father, the Duke of Colebourne, Lucas had paced the hallway. With each step he took, he'd grown more agitated with his father for continuing with his schemes to control who his cousins made for matches.

"Are you still hell-bent on this matchmaking madness?" Lucas demanded, prowling back and forth across the front of the desk.

The duke laughed at his agitated son. His sister-in-law smiled in amusement behind Lucas. His son had made his position clear on Colebourne's matchmaking attempts. At least he had Susanna for a co-conspirator. They worked perfectly together. He knew his late wife, Olivia, would have found the same joy in watching the girls fall in love as he had. If they needed an extra push, far be it for him not to guide them toward their happiness.

"It is not madness, my boy, to see your family settled."

Lucas paused, facing his father. "I think you have interfered enough. Look at what poor Evelyn had to endure because of your interference."

Colebourne nodded. "It built her character and gave her the confidence she needed for her role as a countess."

"You cannot deny the love between Evelyn and Reese. He adores her." Aunt Susanna sighed.

Lucas rolled his eyes. "Now. But not when they first wed. If you had not played games with their courtship, Evelyn and Reese would never have suffered a turbulent start to their marriage."

"Yes, but look at Charlotte and Jasper. They make a lovely couple." Aunt Susanna smiled smugly.

Lucas threw his hands in the air and continued with his pacing. "Scandal tainted each of their unions. No proper gentleman will take a second look upon Jacqueline and Gemma if a single whiff of their ruinations came to light."

"Perhaps a proper gentleman is not what Jacqueline and Gemma need." Colebourne arched his brow.

Lucas shook his head in frustration. "That comment alone signifies your madness."

Colebourne laughed. "You forgot to mention Abigail in your speech."

"We have had this discussion before, Father. You cannot present Abigail to society or to the same gentlemen as Jacqueline and Gemma."

"Nonsense!" cried Susanna. "Why ever not?"

Lucas swung his gaze of disbelief on his aunt. "Not you too?"

"It does not matter. I have already chosen a gentleman for Abigail, and he is most proper. Too proper if you ask for my opinion," muttered Colebourne.

"You have chosen a suitor for Abigail. Who?" growled Lucas.

"Abigail is none of your concern. The only lady you need to worry over is Lady Selina, your betrothed."

"Who is he?" Lucas gritted his teeth.

The duke sat forward in his chair. "The only information I will divulge is that the gentleman comes from an upstanding family. He has shown an interest in our sweet Abigail. I greatly approve of this gentleman. However, it is not their time yet, but soon. For now, Abigail needs to enjoy the opportunity of a season. To form friendships, dance with a bevy of gentlemen, dress in lovely gowns, and perhaps steal a kiss or two. When I deem the moment right, I will make the introductions and allow the courtship to proceed, but not until then."

Lucas placed his fists on the duke's desk. "She will not agree to this plan of yours. Abigail has already stated that after Jacqueline and Gemma get married, she plans to seek employment. While I shall stop that from happening, I will not allow you to parade her around the ton for them to shun her. Do you not have a care for her feelings?"

"No one will dare shun any ward of mine," said Colebourne confidently.

"No, not in plain sight. But they will whisper their dislike." Lucas turned to his aunt. "Tell him."

"Tell him what?" asked Susanna, tilting her head.

"That you do not agree with him."

Susanna shrugged. "But I do. I think his plan is marvelous. Also, I wholeheartedly agree with the gentleman Colebourne approves of for Abigail. They will make a splendid couple."

"You both are mad." Lucas kept shaking his head, trying to grasp how he couldn't make them see reason.

Colebourne and Susanna laughed, which only annoyed Lucas more. They were two peas in a pod. Aunt Susanna agreed with his father's mischief and came up with her own ideas. When they plotted together, their devious minds were no match for anyone.

"I will inform Abigail of your plans," threatened Lucas.

"If you feel that is in her best interest, we cannot stop you," said Colebourne.

Lucas stormed from the room, the same way he entered. Colebourne's cunning smile found Susanna's. They both chuckled their amusement at his expense.

"He will inform Abigail of our plans," warned Susanna.

Colebourne rubbed his hands in glee. "That is what I am hoping for. It is all part of my plan to provoke Abigail into joining Jacqueline and Gemma for the season. My son will aggravate her so much, she will attempt to prove him wrong. Oh, I can see her at the balls now. Every gentleman will line up to ask her to dance."

"In which it will provoke Lucas into a jealous rage." Susanna snickered.

"Exactly. Then the rest of the plan will fall into place."

She cocked an eyebrow. "Do you not mean that the pieces in play will fall into a jumbled mess?"

Colebourne grinned. "Precisely. Then the other players will have to pick up those pieces and play them to the best of their skills."

"You are a very devious opponent, Your Grace."

Colebourne relaxed back in the chair. "One must be devious to achieve victory."

"May I inquire why you did not force the issue with Lady Selina? You cannot put off her father for much longer."

Colebourne drummed his fingers on his desk. "Once Lucas informs Abigail of our discussion and he blunders his attempts to spare her feelings, he will set Abigail in a tiff. That is when I will inform Lucas of the settlement discussion and the date I have chosen for his wedding. Then Lucas will find himself too busy to make amends."

Susanna twisted her lips. "You do not plan for this union to happen, do you?"

"No. That is where I will need your assistance once again."

"Anything," came Susanna's immediate answer.

"I need you to extend an invitation to Duncan. My sources inform me that a scandal surrounds him in Edinburgh. One that, if Duncan does not flee, he will find himself wed to a lass pregnant with another man's child." Colebourne tapped at a letter in front of him.

"Which lass?" Susanna clutched at her pearls.

"She is not important. Duncan arriving in London within the next few weeks is."

Susanna's pensive stare at Colebourne would make most men squirm. However, Colebourne knew her weapons and her weaknesses. Her son, Duncan, was the weakest link in her defense.

"I will extend the invitation today."

Colebourne nodded. "Excellent. I will have a room prepared."

"No. He will stay at our home."

"Nonsense. Why open your townhome when mine has more than enough adequate rooms?" Colebourne watched as Susanna contemplated his question.

For his plan to succeed, he needed Duncan underfoot. Because if he knew his nephew as well as he did, then Duncan wouldn't be able to resist the lovely lady who would join her father in finalizing the marriage settlement.

Susanna's eyes narrowed. "Very well. Do not imagine you are sneaky enough that I do not know the reason you request my son's visit."

Colebourne gave her an innocent look. "I hold no clue to your accusation."

"Yes, keep telling yourself that, Colebourne."

Colebourne smiled. "I could get nothing past Olivia either."

"Our mother taught us well." Susanna smirked.

Colebourne laughed. "That she did."

"I assume from Lord Ralston's visit, Gemma is next?"

"Yes, starting tomorrow night at the Calderwood Ball."

Susanna rose from the chair. "Why the rush?"

"Worthington's brother, Graham, has taken an interest in Gemma. And I suspect Gemma returns the same fascination." Colebourne rose and walked Susanna to the door.

"Yes, I noticed their flirtation at dinner last week."

"Then you understand the need for our immediate matchmaking attempt?" asked Colebourne

"Yes."

Chapter One

"Is he not the most divine?" Gemma Holbrooke sighed to her new friend, Noel Worthington.

"You must stop drooling over my brother. It is most disturbing to listen to," teased Noel.

Gemma turned her head to smirk. "Well, I only speak the truth. Not only divine, but most charming too."

"I will accept the next dance from whoever asks just to get away from your infatuation. You made a promise not to speak of Graham this evening," threatened Noel in a teasing tone.

Gemma heaved a sigh. "I know. But look at him, he is most dreamy. With those blond locks and his bedroom eyes. They are smokey and filled with hidden secrets. I am only curious …"

"Akh," Noel growled, her hands clamping over her ears.

Gemma laughed. "I promise I will stop this instance. No more."

"You promise?" asked Noel.

"Well, for this evening anyhow." Gemma winked.

Noel shook her head at Gemma. It didn't matter anyway. Gemma held no interest in Graham Worthington, other than she enjoyed flirting with him. He was called Worth by his friends. She found pleasure when gentlemen paid attention to her, and with Worth, she didn't have to worry about him wanting anything more than a little fun. She had caught Uncle

Theo's frown over their friendship. Not to mention Worth's brother, Lord Worthington, had warned him away. Evelyn, Gemma's cousin, had married Lord Worthington, and she told Gemma that Worthington didn't approve of a match between her and Worth. Still, she enjoyed herself too much to stop.

"If you must moon over someone, why not him?" With her fan, Noel discreetly indicated the gentleman standing in the ballroom entry.

Gemma's gaze followed Noel's train of thought. Oh, but her friend had no clue how much Gemma mooned over Lord Ralston already. Gemma had made a fool of herself with the gentleman during her uncle's house party. She had thrown herself at the lord, only for him to rebuff her every time she approached him. The last night of the house party, she had followed Lord Ralston into the gardens. When he realized they were alone, he'd ordered her back inside. However, her determination to tempt Lord Ralston to kiss her had only caused him to quicken his pace and return to the ball to lose himself in the crowd. Gemma had searched everywhere, but she hadn't been able to find him. During breakfast the next morning, Gemma learned that Lord Ralston had left during the night.

Barrett Ralston caused Gemma's insides to quiver with longing. Even staring at him now set her on edge.

Gemma's disappointment had lingered until Graham Worthington came into her life, making it bright again. Even though Worth was a dear, Lord Ralston was a temptation she refused to resist. She wondered if she could convince Worth to help her win Lord Ralston's favor. She knew Worth wasn't looking for a relationship. No, he enjoyed his bachelor ways too much to tie himself down. If Worth agreed to help her, then she could fool Uncle Theo into believing her interests lie elsewhere.

Uncle Theo may not like Gemma and Worth's flirtation, but he insisted Gemma stay away from Lord Ralston. It wasn't so much of a declaration of Ralston's unworthiness, but he forbade it. When Uncle Theo forbade anything, it was his final word. Usually, she only had to sweet-talk Uncle Theo, and he relented. But once he issued the word *forbidden*, there was no argument for debate. His decision stayed final.

"I already do. The man is in my dreams every night while I sleep." Gemma sighed.

"Then why do you flirt with my brother? Everyone describes your behavior as smitten."

Gemma twisted her lips. "Because Uncle Theo has forbidden me to even talk to Lord Ralston."

Noel gasped. "Oh, that is a shame."

"Why?"

"Because I would not mind listening to you worship over him. He is every girl's wish." Noel sighed much like Gemma had.

Gemma didn't disagree with her friend. Lord Ralston made every innocent maiden's thoughts border on scandalous. At least her musings did. Even now as she took in his appearance, she dreamed of him wrapping her in his embrace and ravishing her lips. She wanted to run her fingers through Ralston's dark hair that hung near his collar, stare into his mysterious eyes the color of a grey storm brewing, and listen to his devil-may-care attitude. Every word out of his mouth whispered of indecent temptations. He tried shocking Gemma, but he only made her curious to learn if he spoke the truth of his exploits.

"Are Lord Ralston and Worth friends?" Gemma asked, watching the two gentlemen in a discussion.

Noel shrugged. "I would not know. Graham never brings his friends around. Reese does not approve of the lot and does not allow them anywhere near us girls. Mama approves of Reese's decision, and Evelyn is just as protective."

"Mmm, that is a shame. I had hoped to learn more about Lord Ralston." Gemma's gaze stayed focused on the two debonair gentlemen.

"Are you going to disobey Colebourne's demand?" asked Noel.

Gemma turned with a dreamy expression. "Would you if Worthington kept you from the one you love?"

"You love Lord Ralston?" Noel whispered.

"Yes." Gemma smiled

"Oh, how romantic! Was it love at first sight?"

"Yes." Gemma sighed, remembering the first time she saw Lord Ralston.

Noel shook her head. "No, I would not follow the rules either. In fact, since this is all in the name of love, I shall help you any way I can."

Gemma clutched Noel's hands. "You would do that for me?"

Noel nodded, smiling. "Yes."

Gemma squeezed Noel's hands in thanks. Gemma had hoped Abigail would have been the one to offer to help her. But Abigail didn't trust Lord Ralston and agreed with Uncle Theo on staying away from the scoundrel. It didn't help that her cousin Charlotte agreed as well after sitting next to him at dinner one night during the house party.

Abigail was like a sister to her, even though Abigail's mother had been Gemma's mother's maid. But because both of their mothers died in a tragic accident, they'd grown close like sisters. All because of Uncle Theo. He took Abigail in with Gemma and her cousins when their parents died and treated Abigail as one of them. However, her friend remained stubborn about where her place in society was.

Abigail refused to attend the balls and only accepted the invitations where she presented herself as a companion. It was all preposterous. In time, Gemma hoped they could convince her to partake in the season. Gemma's greatest wish was for them to find their soul mates together. However, she feared Abigail had already found hers. And that gentleman was beyond her reach. Not because of his standing in society, but because his father had decided his betrothal when he was but a small lad in leading strings.

"Gemma?" Noel asked.

"Mmm," Gemma murmured, lost in thought.

"Does Lord Ralston know of your uncle's demands?"

"I am not sure. Why?"

Noel's eyes widened. "Because he is walking towards us, and he has not taken his eyes off of you since he entered the ballroom."

Gemma glanced up to see Ralston striding toward them, his intentions clear. Once he reached them, any words she might have spoken got stuck in her throat at the storm brewing in his eyes. Ralston being so near affected Gemma so strongly that she didn't hear what he asked. Noel nudged her elbow, her head tilting toward Ralston, who stood waiting for Gemma's answer.

"Yes," she squeaked.

"Excellent." He held out his hand for Gemma to place her gloved palm in his and led her to the dance floor.

Gemma glanced over her shoulder at Noel, who winked in approval. In her bewilderment, she'd promised herself to dance with Lord Ralston. Her eyes scanned the ballroom to see if her uncle noticed her dance partner. Gemma didn't find Uncle Theo in the crowd, but she spotted her chaperone, Aunt Susanna. However, her aunt was talking in a circle of friends and paid Gemma no attention. Or so she thought.

Gemma tried to relax, but Ralston's very presence made her nerves flutter uncontrollably. Did he notice her fingers tremble? With each turn, he let his touch linger a bit longer. Soon, he whispered near her ear. She couldn't recall what he said. His undivided attention caused her to lose herself in the moment. Ralston probably thought her an odd debutante. However, Gemma held no control over her reactions, no matter how hard she tried to focus. She was hopeless. Perhaps even a bit mad, like Lucas always called her uncle.

Was her reaction to Lord Ralston a sign of madness? If so, it was a madness full of desire.

~~~~~

Barrett Ralston stood inside the entryway to the ballroom, searching for his prey. Once he located her, he stood and took in her beauty. She may have looked like all the other debutantes circling the ball, but the unique aura surrounding her cast a glow.

He shook his head at his poetic gibberish. Aura. Glow. Next, he would quote renditions of Byron on his knee while staring adoringly into her eyes. He needed to get himself together before approaching Gemma Holbrooke.

He must follow through with the Duke of Colebourne's order for this evening. The duke held all his vowels. If he wanted them to disappear, then he must do the duke's bidding. In return, the duke promised not to tell Ralston's father of his gambling debts. While he usually won, he had been on a losing streak lately, stacking up substantial debt wherever he played. The only reason Ralston didn't want his father aware of his gambling was because his father would question the reason behind his philandering ways.

And that was a secret he needed to keep hidden for a while longer.

Colebourne thought he held all the power by forcing Ralston to do his bidding. When, in fact, Colebourne gave him the perfect opportunity for stolen moments with a rare beauty. Colebourne had dragged him away from London when he'd been on a winning streak to work off his debt to attend a house party. Ralston had been furious. It hadn't been just any house party, but one where Colebourne picked each gentleman specifically for one of his wards.

Once the party began in full swing, Ralston set his eyes on Gemma, but the duke informed him that Gemma wasn't for the likes of him. No, he had another gentleman in mind for her. However, that bloke had been unable to attend. Colebourne's only command was to keep Gemma occupied from the other gentlemen so they wouldn't press their courtships on his niece.

Ralston couldn't afford to anger the duke this early in the game. He held all the power. So Ralston had agreed to the duke's orders, biding his time until he got Gemma alone. With a little luck, he could steal her away from prying eyes, if only for a brief spell.

He'd been a fool the one time she'd been within his grasp. She had followed him into the dark garden, and he pretended indifference. Then he fled like a coward before dawn. Her uncle had watched her too closely and would have known if Ralston stole a kiss or two. No, his role was to keep up the pretense of a scoundrel chasing every skirt in sight. As long as it wasn't Gemma.

Gemma Holbrooke.

The moment he caught his first glance, he had fallen victim to love. Love at first sight was foolish…. but was it really? How else could he explain the flood of emotions that consumed him whenever he saw her? Let alone when he was in the same company with her. She had been a permanent fixture in his dreams since the house party. He remembered her greeting the guests with her cousins and her sparkling personality enveloping the room. Whenever he saw her, she had a smile on her face, and he pretended to act bored with her company, when the only emotion coursing through his veins was the thrill of desire.

"Ralston?" Graham Worthington drew his attention away from his obsession, but only for a brief second.

"Worth."

"Who has caught your attention?" Worth followed Ralston's gaze.

"Only looking for my next dance partner. I see Gemma Holbrooke. I should dance with her since I met her at Colebourne's house party. It would only be polite. Or perhaps I shall ask for an introduction to the beauty at her side."

"You will stay clear of that beauty," Worth growled.

"Mmm, chosen her for yourself, have you?" Ralston cocked his eyebrow.

Worth gritted through his teeth. "She is my sister and too pure for the likes of you."

A common theme amongst the fathers and brothers of the ton concerning Ralston. He'd built himself a reputation of a scoundrel of the highest honor. Between his whoring, gambling, drinking, and no respect for society, he was the bad seed of the ton.

Yet, his wildness attracted him to keep receiving invitations to every event. He was also the Duke of Theron's heir, a marquess in his own right. Not a single peer would snub the heir of a duke.

Ralston chuckled. "I understand. If she were my sister, I would deliver you the same warning. Thankfully, they are still in the nursery."

Worth laughed. "That is what I like about you, Ralston. Your sense of humor and your ability to act nonchalant. I can never tell if you mean what you say."

Ralston raised an eyebrow. "Then I guess I have achieved my actual goal. Always keep them wondering."

"Have you taken care of the matter we discussed a few days ago?"

Ralston glanced around to see if anyone was listening. "Yes, the target has taken the bait."

"Excellent. I shall contact you soon for an update."

Ralston nodded. "I guess I will claim the lovely Gemma for the next dance."

"Be careful of that one," Worth warned with a chuckle.

"Why?" Ralston broke his perusal of the lovely blonde to question Worth on his implication.

"She is a lively one and will break your heart with just a smile. Oh, but I forget, you have no heart," Worth joked, slapping Ralston on the back.

It might have been a jest. However, the whole ton whispered of his coldness discard of mistresses, his callous disregard of ruining innocents, and the shameful way he seduced ladies in front of their husbands.

If only Gemma hadn't already stolen his heart. A fact Ralston needed to keep hidden.

He needed to leave Worth's company before he struck the bloke. He didn't like knowing Worth and Gemma flirted with each other. His friend held the same reputation of warming many bedsheets across London.

Ralston shrugged before strolling away to his prey. Worth's sister was whispering to Gemma, causing a warm blush to spread across her cheeks before she lifted her gaze to him. Her hazel eyes grew larger with every step he took. She'd kept her hair down this evening with clasps decorated in tiny pearls behind her ears, and a single pearl on a chain adorned her neck. Her blond hair shone, but the glow from the candlelight hinted at a light reddish tint. Her yellow gown reminded him of a buttercup, simple but elegant.

"May I have this dance?" Ralston stood waiting for his answer to the dance the musicians were preparing for.

Gemma didn't answer him and appeared lost in thought. As her friend tried to get her attention, Ralston's spirits sank. She didn't wish to dance with him after all. He had been confident of her answering yes. Even Colebourne had insisted Gemma would dance with him if he asked. Colebourne wanted who he chose for a groom to see that one of the ton's rakehells had his sight set on Gemma for his next conquest. Colebourne hoped the gentleman would rescue Gemma from Ralston's clutches.

When Gemma laid her hand in his, he breathed a sigh of relief. Her hand trembled in his. At every chance, he let his fingers caress her longer. He never meant to seduce her during this dance. But Worth's comments spurred Ralston to start his seduction of Gemma Holbrooke.

"I wish to steal a kiss from your sweet lips," he whispered into her ear as he spun her around.

Gemma stumbled, and he caught her closer to him. She raised her startled gaze to his. He expected a shocked reply to his indecent comment, but to his surprise, her eyes sparked with an unspoken desire. One he needed to explore this instant.

They were near the end of the dance line, and the crowd had grown near them. No one would notice if they slipped out the doors that led to the balcony. He glanced around the ballroom, searching for Colebourne and Lady Forrester, Gemma's chaperone.

"They are not watching," Gemma whispered.

At her soft words, Ralston lost his concern for Gemma's reputation. The temptation to steal a kiss overruled his common sense. They may not have their eyes upon them, but Ralston knew what they risked if Colebourne discovered their indiscretion. However, Gemma removed any of the doubts he harbored when she tugged on his hand.

This was madness, but he no longer cared. They could lock him away. If he stole one moment with Gemma, it would be worth it.

Ralston needed no other encouragement. He led them out onto the dark balcony and around to a display of plants, the perfect hiding spot. Shame overcame Ralston at having knowledge of all the secret hiding places at every home in London, where he had stolen many widows, debutantes, and married women away for secret trysts.

However, this evening was different. Or so he kept telling himself. This tryst was different. Gemma was different. How he felt toward Gemma and the time they spent together meant more to him.

Any other time, his confidence controlled his actions. He dominated their senses and seduced them with whispered words and stolen kisses, promising them more if they allowed him a few favors to tide him over. Now, his confidence fled, and he was a bundle of nerves. He feared he would scare her away with his forwardness. Ralston lost all sense of who he was when he stood in Gemma's presence.

Once he secured a hiding spot, Ralston drew Gemma into his embrace. He swung her around, pressing her back against the stone wall. He lowered his head and paused, their lips but a breath apart, and waited.

Gemma's lips trembled, and her tongue darted out to wet her lips. He growled. His thumb traced the path of her tongue, pulling a moan from between her lips. He leaned down and brushed his lips once, twice against hers, before his mouth devoured the sweet nectar of temptation. Gemma opened at his demand, and he left her with no mercy.

"You taste so exquisite," Ralston moaned in between kisses.

Gemma clung to Ralston, holding on for dear life. The power of his kisses drugged her senses, leaving her floating. He pushed his body into hers, and the brick scraped against her back. However, she felt no pain but only the sheer pleasure of heaven.

Ralston probably thought her an innocent miss since she never moved, but she was powerless to the sensation. The first gentle brush of his mouth stunned her. Then he ravished her, and Gemma's need awakened her to return his kisses with her own. To leave the same mark on Ralston that he left on her.

She pressed her chest against his, her hands diving into his hair. Her fingers gripped the soft waves, holding him to her. When Ralston's tongue stroked against hers, Gemma gave as good as she got. With each bold touch, Ralston moaned his pleasure along with her sighs. Each time they pulled away to draw a breath, an ache consumed her until he dominated her with more kisses. Each one was more relentless than the last.

Gemma expected a rake as experienced as Ralston to try more than sensuous kisses. His hands stayed firmly wrapped around her, keeping her close to him. Was she too innocent for him? She didn't hold a candle to his other conquests. However, their kisses and the proof of his desire pressing into her middle spoke otherwise.

Why did he attempt nothing more?

Her kisses drove Ralston to the brink of madness. He never wanted to stop. However, he must. If he didn't return Gemma to the ballroom before the dance was over, they risked getting caught. Then she wouldn't get to enjoy the season because of him. He may be a selfish bastard, but he refused to be Gemma's downfall. She wasn't his yet. Until she was, he refused to allow scandal to touch her.

Her soft lips melted under his, and her purrs of satisfaction echoed in his ears. He ached to take her. Oh, how much he desired to lift her dress around her hips and plow into her. But he refused to slake his urges as he had on other ladies in the past. No. Their first time making love would only leave them with enchanted memories. Memories they would fill with a lifetime of finding pleasure with each other.

And no duke would stand between them.

With much reluctance, he pulled away and reached up to pull her hands from his hair. When her eyes clouded with the loss and her mouth formed into a pout, Ralston growled his own disappointment. The fool that he was, he stole one more kiss before stepping away. He didn't stray too far, only far enough so they could no longer touch. He needed to keep his sanity. This was unfamiliar terrain he ventured in, so out of the ordinary from his usual trysts. However, he refused to label this as a tryst. No, it was a stolen moment with a lady who held his heart in the palm of her hand. She may not realize the power she held, but Ralston gifted her with a trust he'd never held for another.

"I … ahh … that is …" Ralston stumbled out an apology.

"Shh," Gemma whispered, stopping him.

"I need to—"

"No, please don't." Gemma's voice trembled.

Ralston raked his hand through his hair in frustration. He wanted to express himself, but he turned into a bumbling fool who couldn't voice his emotions. If he were whispering words of seduction, it would be another story.

Gemma stood before him on the verge of tears, misunderstanding their time spent alone. He wanted to reassure her the kisses were special. Instead, she probably thought what everyone else thought of him.

Why would Gemma be any different? He should have slacked his desires with seduction. After a few more caresses, Gemma Holbrooke would have spread her thighs like all the other conquests he had seduced in darkened corners. Except she was of a different class. Ralston only had himself to blame for tainting their first kiss with reminders from his past.

Before he could react, Gemma slipped under his arm and left him hidden behind the plants. He watched her run across the balcony and didn't follow. It was for the best. If he followed, he would have to explain himself. And he had no explanation, other than the dire need to hold her in his arms with her mouth beneath his. He watched her stop before she reached the light coming from the balcony doors. She wiped the tears from her eyes and gathered herself.

"Turn around," Ralston begged. "Please turn."

However, Gemma didn't hear his whispered pleas or else she refused to acknowledge them. Ralston would never know. Whatever he had hoped to achieve burned to ashes at his feet. He'd blown any opportunity he had with her when he didn't reassure her how much the kiss meant to him. He wanted to follow Gemma to see her reaction, but he needed to leave for his own protection.

Because when, not if, the duke learned of his niece sneaking away from the dance with him, Ralston didn't want to be anywhere near Colebourne's wrath. Then the duke would rescind his offer for Ralston to work off his debt. The duke would demand payment. A substantial amount of blunt that Ralston didn't have but soon would.

~~~~~~

Gemma lay in bed, trying to fall asleep but to no avail. Barrett Ralston and his devouring kisses consumed her thoughts. The images of them kissing flashed more vividly when she closed her eyes. Her lips still tingled from where he'd traced them with his thumb, and later with his mouth. Her body burned from pressing against him. His onslaught of kisses awakened Gemma from a simple infatuation to a woman on the brink of having her every desire fulfilled. She lay aching for him. She didn't understand her body's needs, but Ralston would know how to ease her quivering flesh.

Does he ache for me the same? Gemma wondered.

Gemma kept trying to answer the question since he'd pulled away from their kisses. The distance he put between them had been more than obvious. When he tried to apologize, Gemma had stopped him. She hadn't wanted the stolen moment ruined with regrets. She held none, and she prayed Ralston didn't either.

Gemma had paused near the entrance to the ballroom. She wanted to turn around to see if he followed. When the air remained still behind her, she knew he hadn't. However, their connection never severed. Gemma felt Ralston watching her, and with that, her smile grew wide, and she strolled inside the ballroom with an innocent look of a debutante who only stepped outside for a brief spell. The dance ended, and she got caught up in the crowd, making her explanation for being alone more believable. She'd explained to Aunt Susanna that she got separated from her dance partner in the crowd. Gemma blathered on about how she hoped she didn't commit a faux pas and offend her dance partner. Her chaperone assured her it was a regular occurrence whenever a ball was a success.

Gemma held no guilt for her lies. To do so would mean she regretted sneaking away with Ralston. She would do so again if an opportunity presented itself. Perhaps she could hold his interest for longer than a few kisses…

Gemma then realized what she needed to capture Ralston's undivided attention. She needed to make herself irresistible to him. What better way than to flirt with him whenever their paths crossed.

Gemma smiled at her plan, closed her eyes, and let the memory of Ralston's kisses lead her into dreamland.

Chapter Two

Gemma sat next to Abigail during breakfast the next morning and described the ball. They usually gathered in one of their bedrooms in the morning for scones and hot chocolate. However, while they were in town, Uncle Theo requested their attendance on the mornings after the entertainments to discuss how they fared. On the evenings they spent at home, they could continue with their morning ritual.

Abigail asked Gemma about the dancing and the dresses the ladies wore. Gemma hoped that if she made the entertainments exciting enough, Abigail would join them for the season's activities. While Gemma had enjoyed herself immensely last night, it hadn't been the same without her best friend.

"Did I see you dancing with Lord Ralston?" asked Uncle Theo.

The room grew quiet while everyone waited for Gemma to answer. Everyone knew of Uncle Theo forbidding Gemma from socializing with Lord Ralston, and on the first ball Gemma attended, she'd gone against his wishes. However, she was confident her uncle wouldn't find fault with her excuse.

She sat down her cup of tea and folded her hands in her lap before turning toward her uncle. "Yes."

"May I ask why?" Uncle Theo attempted to ask in a stern voice, but Gemma's smile always softened him from treating her too harshly.

"I could not refuse him while the other guests observed. It would have appeared as if I snubbed him. Aunt Susanna taught me that one cannot refuse the heir to a duke and walk away unscathed. Then society would deem me unapproachable. I thought your greatest wish was for me to find a suitor you would approve of for a courtship. If I danced with a duke's son, then other gentlemen would extend many plentiful offers." Gemma took a sip of tea.

Aunt Susanna tried soothing over the duke's displeasure. "She has a point, Theodore. Not that Gemma needed Ralston's invitation to dance. Gemma and Jaqueline were belles of the ball. They were both introduced to and danced with many promising gentlemen. I heard many whispers of interest. When the parlor fills with callers soon, it will come as no surprise."

Colebourne's eyes narrowed. "I will concede. However, I will not tolerate this to become a regular occurrence. Especially since I couldn't find you after a few turns. Can you explain your absence from the dance floor?"

Gemma spread some jam on her scone. "I only snuck outside to draw a quick breath of fresh air after the set and immediately stepped right back in. I got lost in the crowd from Lord Ralston before he could escort me back to Aunt Susanna." She raised her gaze to her uncle.

"Mmm," Colebourne murmured.

Her uncle's skeptical stare made Gemma want to squirm in her seat. But if she did, it would show proof of her lies. Then her uncle would have her every action observed and reported back to him.

Gemma glanced at Jaqueline for help in changing the course of the conversation. But her cousin avoided her look, pretending interest with her breakfast. While Jaqueline had only picked at her plate, pushing her food around before Uncle Theo's questioning, now she ate heartily. Gemma narrowed her gaze. Jaqueline was acting suspiciously herself.

Then Gemma recalled Jacqueline had been absent from the ball too. She saw Jacqueline accept a dance with Lord Kincaid before her own dance with Lord Ralston.

However, Jaqueline never returned until two dances later, pleading she had been in the waiting room having her dress repaired. A dress which still looked immaculate. Not as immaculate as Jaqueline herself though. She'd appeared flushed and out of breath, with a few strands of her hair loosened from her coiffure.

Gemma's eyes widened with the realization that her cousin had snuck away for her own tryst. Had she been with Lord Kincaid? Or had another gentleman paid attention to Jacqueline and Gemma had failed to notice?

Either way, they both stood on the edge of ruining their reputations. They may be wards of a duke, but they didn't hold the same standing in society had they been his daughters.

She didn't want to draw any attention toward Jacqueline. Jacqueline, above all others in her family, deserved love. She was the eldest and had put her feelings aside, acting motherly when Aunt Susanna wasn't around. She dried their tears, listened to their dreams, and held them when they needed comforting. Recently, both of Jacqueline's sisters had fallen in love, and she deserved to find the same destiny. Lord Kincaid would be the perfect suitor for Jacqueline. Gemma liked him. She hoped he was the gentleman, but if he wasn't, then as long as Jacqueline loved her mystery suitor and he loved her too, that was all that mattered.

Gemma turned her gaze back to her uncle, offering him a smile of innocence. "Did you enjoy yourself at the ball, Uncle Theo? I noticed the widow Hadley smiling at you."

Colebourne huffed. "You know I pay no attention to other ladies. Your Aunt Olivia still holds my heart. However, yes, it was an enjoyable evening, watching you young ladies twirl around the dance floor. Now, if only we can convince Abigail to join in the festivities."

Gemma's intention wasn't to direct her uncle's attention toward Abigail. She understood why her friend wasn't comfortable with her entrance into society. But Uncle Theo's wish was the same as hers. Perhaps if Aunt Susanna invited the girls from the house party over for tea, Abigail would find comfort in how much they accepted her.

Abigail sat her napkin next to her plate and smiled at Uncle Theo. "If you will please excuse me." She made no explanation, only smiling wistfully at them before leaving.

"Father, why do you insist on making it uncomfortable for Abigail? She has made her stand clear. Why can you not accept it?" growled Lucas.

"Because her excuses are foolish," answered Colebourne.

"Perhaps to you. But not to her. And I, for one, agree with Abigail," argued Lucas.

Jacqueline narrowed her gaze at Lucas. "Why?"

"Do you hold the opinion that Abigail is not worthy enough? Charlie hinted at your cruelty towards Abigail," accused Gemma.

Colebourne leaned back in his chair, smiling in enjoyment at the attack on Lucas. His son would never learn when to keep his opinions to himself. He had a lot to teach his son before Lucas became a duke. For now, Colebourne would watch how he handled not one but three irritated ladies at the breakfast table. If he came out unscathed, then Lucas had better negotiation skills than Colebourne gave him credit for.

Aunt Susanna set her cup down. "Lucas, I believe your cousins have asked you some questions. Questions I wish to hear the answers to myself."

Lucas blew out his breath in frustration, realizing how he'd offended Abigail yet again. Not that he meant offense. He only faced reality where the rest of his family denied it. He watched his father enjoy his predicament, not helping him to explain why allowing Abigail to enter the marriage mart was the same as throwing her into a pit of sharks. There were the jealous ladies who felt like they had earned their place because of their rank in the peerage to the fortune hunters seeking an innocent miss to con. Then there were the lords who would consider Abigail a tasty treat to amuse themselves with. Her standing left her vulnerable to the vultures. Lucas only wanted to protect Abigail from every distasteful incident that would present itself once she stepped foot amongst the ton.

Lucas cleared his throat. "Abigail is more than worthy to enjoy a season in London. However, it is most improper, and I worry she will get hurt at the chilly reception she will encounter. I only wish to protect her. As for what Charlie perceived to have overheard, she misunderstood my reasons on why I believe this is not a wise idea. That is why one should not eavesdrop. They do not listen to the full conversation, only the parts they wish to hear."

"Is the reason you wish to keep Abigail from falling in love with another gentleman because you want her for yourself?" Everyone grew still at Jacqueline's question. Each of them believed her question held the truth, but they waited for Lucas to admit to it.

Lucas narrowed his gaze toward Jacqueline. "You are out of line with your question, cousin. I only wish the best for Abigail, as do all of us. I am honor bound to marry Selina Pemberton."

"You evaded my question, but I will not press for an answer. I only want you to consider the real reason you wish to deny Abigail this chance. If you cannot be honest with us, at least be honest with yourself," Jacqueline said before she rose and left.

Gemma watched Lucas storm out of the room behind Jacqueline, heading in the opposite direction. She didn't understand why Jacqueline pressed the issue for Lucas to admit to his feelings for Abigail. It would prove nothing, only heartache for her friend. Gemma knew Abigail had secretly loved Lucas since they moved in with Uncle Theo. Abigail saw Lucas as her hero.

Lucas had been the one to make Abigail feel accepted into their family when they were younger. They shared a kinship, loving the same books and taking long walks in the countryside. Their viewpoints on politics ran along the same line. If not, Lucas listened to Abigail's opinions with an open mind. They were perfect for each other.

But Lucas was out of her reach, and the closer Lucas's announcement of his nuptials drew, the more distance Abigail put between them. Their friendly conversations ceased to exist because of their frequent arguments. Only Selina could break the betrothal. And that witch would never relinquish her connection to Lucas and the power she would hold once Lucas became a duke. Gemma wondered if there were another way to break the betrothal.

"Do not think I have forgotten about Lord Ralston, young lady," Uncle Theo stated, scaring Gemma out of her musings.

Gemma smiled sweetly.

Colebourne laughed. "Nor will your smiles help."

Gemma lifted a shoulder. "It does not hurt to try. Is that not what you always said I should do?"

Aunt Susanna joined in the laughter. "So true. She knows you well, Colebourne."

"That she does. It is what makes her so dangerous." Uncle Theo winked at Gemma.

Chapter Three

Gemma sat between Abigail and Jacqueline during the musical. She didn't understand why her friend had accepted the invitation to attend, but she wouldn't question Abigail in case she changed her mind again. She wanted Abigail to enjoy the season with her.

Gemma turned her head to smile at Abigail, and she returned the gesture. However, it wasn't Abigail's usual smile, but one filled with sadness. Gemma wished for Abigail to confide in her, but would wait until she did. For now, she found comfort in the steps her friend took to find happiness.

Gemma closed her eyes when the melody of the music struck a harmony in her soul. The singer's haunting song told a story of a forbidden love ending in tragedy. It was a story of two lovers who thought they could change the course of their destiny when they succumbed to their desires, only for others to snuff out their passion with their demands. The lyrics resonated in Gemma. She wondered how it would feel to rebel against the demands placed on her if she gave into her desires with Lord Ralston. Would her uncle stop their union? Or would he allow her the chance to make her own mistakes? Were the feelings she held for Lord Ralston a mistake?

When the singer hit a high note that encapsulated her pain, a shiver chased along Gemma's spine. Her eyes flicked open, and she searched the room. All the guests had their attention fixated on the performance—except for one.

Lord Ralston's gaze focused on Gemma, revealing his own desires. The memory of their kiss flashed before her, replaying the passion that had consumed them over and over. When Gemma's eyes locked with Ralston, heat slithered across the room and scorched Gemma in her seat.

Gemma smiled at him, and he whispered into the lady's ear who sat next to him. Gemma frowned when she noticed his companion. The lady needed no introduction. She nodded her acceptance to Ralston's whisper. Then Ralston abruptly left.

The singer finished her song, and the guests rose from their seats to socialize before the second half of the evening's performance.

"I am going to step outside for some fresh air," Gemma mumbled to Abigail.

Gemma lost herself in the throng, following where Ralston had made his departure. She caught the end of his coattails when he rounded the corner. Gemma followed at a discreet distance, glancing over her shoulder to see if anyone watched her. She saw the guests deep in their conversations and none of her family searched for her. Gemma quickened her pace and continued after him as he entered a room at the end of the hall. She paused, placing her ear against the door to listen if he was alone. However, before she heard anything, he wrenched the door open and dragged her inside. The door closed, and Ralston pressed her against it.

"Why did you follow me?" he whispered near her ear.

Gemma shivered, not from fear, but from excitement she tried to contain. The next words she whispered were filled with false bravery, but they held the truth of what she desired the most. "To steal another kiss."

"Oh, God. Do not speak so."

"Why ever not?"

His grip tightened. "Because you hold no clue how your innocent claim can destroy your future."

Gemma licked her lips. "How so?"

"Because you would spend the rest of your life in misery if I gave into the temptation and anyone caught us alone."

"How so?" Gemma asked again, batting her eyelashes.

His gaze stayed fixated on her lips. Ralston moaned. "God, you are so innocent."

"Do you not enjoy my kisses? Or do you prefer a kiss from a more experienced lady? Perhaps the type of kiss your companion this evening can tempt you with."

His jaw ticked. "My preference of kisses is not up for discussion. Your return to the musical without getting caught is," he growled.

"So, you will not kiss me again?" She dragged her teeth across her lower lip.

Ralston shook his head. "No. The kiss we shared at the Calderwood Ball was a mistake. One I cannot afford to make again."

"Is it because of my uncle?"

Ralston released his hold and gently nudged Gemma to the side before he opened the door. Once he calmed his fear that no one had followed her, he opened the door wider, allowing her room to exit. Gemma stomped her foot. She wasn't one to give into tantrums. She usually got her way with sweetness, but Ralston seemed immune to her charm.

Little did Gemma know, Ralston found her charm most enchanting. His gaze had stayed focused on her for the entire performance. She captivated his attention when she closed her eyes and swayed her body to the music. Lady Langdale had kept whispering indecent promises in his ear, trying to tempt him into finding a private room for her to demonstrate her skills. The widow was hunting for another benefactor after Worthington tossed her aside to remain faithful to his bride. Worthington's bride was also Gemma's cousin.

Ralston had accepted the widow's invitation to join him at the musical once he learned Gemma's family also accepted the invitation. His infatuation with the blond-haired beauty would be his downfall, but he found it hard to stay away from her. Now he needed to convince her to leave before Colebourne caught them together. He dreaded the consequences that would befall him if he ruined her.

The duke wouldn't force marriage. No, the duke had made his point clear that he'd chosen another gentleman for Gemma. No matter how many kisses they shared, it would be another gentleman who would enjoy the pleasure of bedding her after they pledged their vows.

But...would one more stolen kiss make much of a difference? The duke was clueless about the other stolen kisses. What would a few more matter?

When Gemma pressed the door closed and took a step closer, her determination rang clear. Ralston was powerless to deny her. It would appear he would have the pleasure of kissing her once again, but would he have the strength to stop after he started?

"Ralston?" Gemma questioned, laying her hand on his chest.

Ralston moaned at how her touch set him on fire. He pulled her to him, crushing her against his chest with her hand trapped. When his head lowered, he ravished the innocent lady in his arms. His mouth pulled kiss after hungry kiss from her lips, demanding her to fall victim to the same passion consuming him. When she opened her mouth under his and whimpered her need, Ralston's desire grew relentless. His tongue stroked and danced with hers.

She slid her hand around his neck and pressed his head closer to hers. Her own mouth made demands that he gladly met. Ralston's hands explored her softness, his thumb brushing across the hardened buds of nipples he wished to devour. When his hand lowered past the softness and pressed into her core, Ralston claimed her whimpered cries.

He ached to lift her skirts and discover if Gemma was wet for him. If he sank his fingers into her desires, would she demand more like she demanded from his kisses?

Ralston bit her bottom lip before kissing a path along her neck, then back to her ear. His fingers rubbed around in circles, causing her ache to grow.

"Are you wet for me, sweet Gemma? Do you want my mouth on your sweet cunny, licking your most wanted desires?" Ralston tempted Gemma with crudity, hoping she would run. Because if she didn't, he would lose any remaining sense of sanity he barely held onto.

He bent his head, and his lips found a pebble poking from her dress and sucked greedily through the thin material. A heady haze of pleasure clouded his judgment to where he only desired to take Gemma Holbrooke against the door.

"I want to strip your dress down and feast on these sweet cherries. Suck them until you cry your pleasure for everyone to hear. Then I want your legs wrapped around my waist while I plow into your precious pussy over and over, taking what I demand."

Ralston kissed away Gemma's gasp, plundering her mouth with his tongue, staking his claim. He hoped his shocking words would cause her to push him away. She must return to the musical before he made good on his word. If she gave any sign that she welcomed his desires, Ralston would lose control.

He bit her earlobe. "Shall we, my love, ease the ache consuming our souls with carnal delights? I promise you will enjoy it."

Gemma needed to stop Ralston before he went any further. His shocking words stunned her, but her body welcomed his warm mouth. She only wanted to guide his lips to where her body ached the most. If his words and kisses were any hint to where their tryst could lead, it held nothing to the caress of his fingers that tantalized her into agreeing to his scandalous offer.

What would it feel like to free herself from her inhibitions and enjoy the pleasure of his promises? She ached to explore this desire they shared… but she must put a stop to this madness before anyone came upon them.

She wanted him for a husband. However, she didn't want her uncle to force Ralston to wed her. Gemma held no doubt her uncle would. Uncle Theo had made his point clear, Gemma was to steer clear of Ralston, and she now understood why. The man was a walking seduction. Gemma promised herself to leave after one more kiss.

Ralston sensed Gemma trying to decide and knew when she came to her decision. Her lips stilled under his for a brief second before she took control of the kiss. Gemma's inexperience endeared her more. Her tongue stroked his lips before sliding inside his mouth to run across his tongue. The kiss was soft. Slow. Intoxicating. Ralston ached for Gemma to never stop her wonderful torment.

When he thought she would continue the pleasurable act, she pulled away. With trembling hands, she straightened her gown and patted her hair into place. Once again, she was an untouchable princess he'd soiled with his indecent ways. She may have tried to make herself appear unapproachable, but now he knew what passion lay underneath her innocent appearance. A passion he would unleash. No other would enjoy the pleasure of Gemma Holbrooke. He no longer cared that Colebourne had forbidden him from her. Their paths had crossed for a reason.

"While I would love to take you up on your scintillating offer, I must refuse. A mere tryst to satisfy your needs is not what I desire. I would much rather prefer a bed and uninterrupted countless hours for the first time we make love." Her innocent smile conflicted with her scandalous remark.

Ralston scoffed. "Who said anything about making love? I only seek to slay my desires between your thighs and nothing more."

Gemma's declaration scared Ralston into continuing his scoundrel meanderings. He didn't mean a word of it. While he had hoped he didn't scare her, she scared him.

"So you say, my love," Gemma said, patting Ralston on the chest, placating him.

"Gemma—"

The door shoved opened, and Ralston slammed it shut with his hand. He placed his foot against the bottom to prevent the person on the other side from discovering them.

"Ralston," Worth hissed through the door. "Are you in there? Is Gemma Holbrooke with you?"

Gemma gasped, embarrassed her new friend had caught her indiscretion.

"Get lost," Ralston growled.

"Damn you! Why would you risk her reputation? Evelyn and Charlotte are waiting at the end of the hall, Gemma. You only have a few more minutes before you find your reputation ruined."

Gemma reached out to pull Ralston's arm from the door and motioned for him to remove his foot. When he stepped back, she offered another smile before opening the door a crack. "Hello, Worth."

"Hello, Gemma. Will you allow me to escort you to your cousins?"

"Yes, I would love your company. Can you please give me one second?"

Worth sighed. "One second, no longer."

"Thank you, Worth, for understanding."

Gemma closed the door and turned toward Ralston. Her innocent smile fooled him no longer. She was a devious witch in disguise. A temptress enflaming his desires. A seductive siren sent to destroy his sanity.

She stood on her tiptoes and kissed his cheek. "Thank you," she whispered before slipping into the hallway.

Thank you? What in the hell was she thanking him for? He threatened to ruin Gemma with her family who was but a few feet away. If Worth hadn't interrupted them, Ralston wouldn't have stopped if Gemma continued kissing him. She might have kissed him like an innocent, but her body told a different story. His crude words only enticed Gemma to discover the truth of his character.

He grew weary of playing the scoundrel with not a care for another. The rumors of his carousing, gambling, drinking, and wild exploits were that: only rumors. He longed to be the gentleman his mother had raised him to be. Instead, he carried the persona of a rake who seduced any lady who crossed his path.

He raised his head when the door clicked open and shut behind him. Had Gemma returned? He turned and stared into the thunderous gaze of Worth. His partner in crime. Ralston realized what he risked by staying alone with Gemma, but he no longer cared. He wanted this latest assignment finished so he could pursue her, with or without Colebourne's permission.

Ralston raised up his hand before Worth could lecture him. "I am aware of what I have risked."

Worth pierced Ralston with his gaze. "Do you?"

"Yes."

"Then why pursue Gemma Holbrooke when you arrived with your mark?"

Ralston ran his hands through his hair, stalking across the room. "I didn't pursue Gemma. She followed me. I only stepped away to clear my head. The next I know, Gemma is in my arms. I couldn't stop, even if I wanted to."

Worth shook his head. "Then I am glad I showed up when I did."

"Thank you for saving my arse once again."

"As of lately, it has been one too many times. Where is your head? Do you not understand we are on the verge of losing whatever we have gained?"

"Yes." Ralston sighed, sinking into a chair. "Did Gemma return to her family without her whereabouts questioned?"

"Yes. However, next time she might not be so lucky." Worth sighed.

"Did anyone notice her absence?"

"Only her cousins. Reese and Sinclair kept Colebourne occupied while their wives searched for Gemma."

Ralston nodded. "And is the widow wondering where I have taken myself off to?"

Worth rolled his eyes. "No. That is another sad state of affairs that my brother is trying to stay clear from. Why did you escort Lady Langdale to this event? Do you not remember she is my brother's ex-mistress?"

Ralston tapped his fingers on the arm of the chair. "I recall Lady Langdale's relationship with Worthington. However, Lady Mitchel invited her to this affair. Whether or not I came with her, she still would have attended. Your brother cannot avoid the widow. They run in the same circles. Plus, I want to end this farce as soon as possible. She has possession of the coin. When I convince her of my attention, she will part with it after a little persuasion. Once I return the coin to Colebourne, he will clear my debt."

"Then you can what? Pursue Gemma when Colebourne has stated his refusal of allowing a courtship to blossom between you? I am afraid not." Worth shook his head.

"You underestimate my power of persuasion, my friend." Ralston narrowed his gaze. "Or are you warning me away from Gemma because you want her for yourself?"

Worth blew out a breath. "No, because I do not wish to see Colebourne strike his wrath in your direction. I rely too much on our partnership for my income. If you pursue Gemma, Colebourne will destroy you and anyone connected with you. Even though my brother married his niece and joined our families together, he will seek his revenge when he discovers we double-crossed him. If you destroy all the progress we have made because you cannot keep your cock in your trousers, then I cannot make the purchase we discussed. Of all the debutantes, why Gemma Holbrooke?"

"I cannot explain. Do not worry though. I will claim the coin and square my debt with Colebourne. Then you and I can pursue our dream. I promise Colebourne will be none the wiser of my pursuit of his niece."

"How will you make that happen?"

Ralston rose and slapped Worth on the back. "Why, with your help."

"No," growled Worth.

"I only need you to pretend an interest in the lady."

"No."

Ralston's smile grew wider. "Then cover for us when the opportunity arises."

"No." Worth gritted his teeth.

"Then everything will fall into place. I will show Colebourne I am worthy of Gemma and he will give his approval."

Worth kept shaking his head in refusal. "No!"

Ralston arched his brow. "Yes. Or else I come clean with Colebourne, Worthington, and the dear widow."

Worth narrowed his eyes. "You wouldn't."

Ralston shrugged. "Wouldn't I?"

"You are a conniving bastard," Worth sneered.

"Your insult offends my mother's honor. You know I am the legitimate heir to the Duke of Theron." Ralston laughed.

Ralston strolled to the door, not waiting for Worth's response. He knew his friend would follow along with his plan for the financial gain he would reap. Soon, Worth fell into step beside him and drew Ralston into a heated debate. When they neared the crowd walking back into the musical, heads turned their way in curiosity of their raised voices.

Ralston noticed and nodded to the widow waiting near the open doors. "I am afraid we must continue our argument later, Mr. Worthington. I must return to Lady Langdale."

Worth nodded and returned to his own family who was waiting nearby.

"Lady Langdale, I am sorry for my time away. I am afraid Mr. Worthington wanted to discuss the merits of the latest bill in Parliament. Even though we do not have a vote, our debates often turn heated. Please accept my apology."

"I will allow you to make it up to me later, my lord," the widow whispered.

"With pleasure," Ralston purred with a wink.

He glanced up at that moment and caught the hurt in Gemma's gaze. He couldn't soothe her wounded emotions without falling out of character. It was for the best that his actions caused her heartache. In time, he would explain. If she expressed her distaste for his character, then Colebourne would lower his guard and make his seduction easier. He arched a brow at Gemma as he wrapped his arm around the widow's waist and guided her back to their seats.

Gemma fumed at the attention Ralston paid toward the widow. The same widow who had been the former mistress for her cousin Evelyn's husband. Was Lady Langdale now Ralston's mistress?

Once Worth delivered Gemma into her cousins' care, she had to endure their lecture at stealing away with a rake. Gemma listened with half an ear, watching for Ralston to return. Her absence went unnoticed by her uncle because of Charlotte's devious thinking. Charlotte threatened to have a discussion of Gemma's behavior tomorrow morning over scones and hot chocolate.

Gemma stalked away, intending to return to her seat when the widow Ralston accompanied cornered her near the door with a threat. "Do not think you can keep a gentleman like Ralston satisfied, my dear. A man with his sexual appetites only seeks pleasure with an experienced lady such as me."

"I have no interest in Lord Ralston. You are mistaken to think otherwise." Gemma looked upon Lady Langdale with disinterest.

"Mmm, I do not think I am. Your absence along with his did not go unnoticed by me, nor does the fullness of your lips. If I am not mistaken, Lord Ralston wears your shade of lip color on his lips. I did not get the chance to warn your cousin away, but I shall with you. I mean to claim Lord Ralston as my next conquest and no Holbrooke chit will stand in my way again. Do I make myself clear, Lady Gemma?" Lady Langdale gritted her teeth behind her false smile.

Gemma raised her chin, narrowing her eyes, before she looked the widow up and down. With a *humph*, she walked away with a nerve she didn't know she possessed. Aunt Susanna had warned them of the vultures of the ton, but Gemma had paid no heed to her warning. Her entire life, she had only encountered generous souls. Now, after confronting a vindictive character, Gemma realized she could handle them with the spiritedness of a Holbrooke. Years of dealing with Selina Pemberton helped to prepare her for the likes of Lady Langdale.

Gemma spent the second half of the musical enjoying the performance. Her gaze never strayed once toward Ralston and his new conquest. Gemma hadn't mistaken the passion she shared with Ralston, and sensed he felt the same. He might have tried to scare her away with his vulgar tongue, but Gemma didn't frighten easily. Nor did the widow's threats scare her. She may be inexperienced, but Ralston craved her. His kisses spoke of the passion he kept contained. Gemma smiled at the pleasure she would enjoy once she brought Ralston to his knees. He wouldn't even see her coming.

As for the widow Langdale, it would appear another Holbrooke chit would ruin her plans once again.

Chapter Four

Gemma curled under the quilt, trying to grab a few more minutes of sleep. She had been on the verge of recapturing her dream when her cousins and Abigail invaded her bedroom.

Ralston's mouth hovered over her lips to kiss her again....

Charlie bounced on the bed, chasing thoughts of Ralston away. "Wake up, dear cousin. It is confession time."

"Why are you here? Uncle Theo will expect us at breakfast for a detailed account of the musical." Gemma moaned into the pillow.

"Evelyn sweet-talked him into agreeing to our morning ritual. She professed how homesick she is for our company and he agreed," explained Abigail.

"Are you?" Gemma lifted her head. She thought her cousin had found bliss in her marriage to Worthington. Perhaps she'd misjudged Evelyn's feelings. "Is everything well with Worthington?"

"Never better." Evelyn sighed.

Gemma's brows drew together. "Oh, then why pretend otherwise?"

"Because we are eager to hear your explanation about your disappearance last night. It is the least you can offer since we covered for you," declared Charlie.

"Gemma, please tell us you did not sneak away with Ralston?" pleaded Abigail.

"No ..." Gemma denied when Charlie exclaimed otherwise.

Charlie smiled mischievously. "She did."

Gemma threw the covers back over her head. She couldn't face them. They were aware of Uncle Theo's threat and would abide by his wishes. She didn't want to disappoint her family. But she couldn't deny what her heart wished for either. And her heart not only wished for but demanded Barrett Ralston.

When a servant carried a tray of scones and hot chocolate into the bedroom, Charlie bounced off the mattress. Gemma heard Abigail and her cousins settle in with food and drink. She remained under the covers, refusing to come out. However, her absence didn't prevent them from discussing Gemma's scandalous tryst.

"I had wondered where she wandered off to," said Abigail.

"I assumed she needed to use the powder room," stated Jacqueline.

"If so, she got lost along the way." Charlie snickered. "Not to mention, her appearance was a bit ruffled when she reappeared. Is that how you would describe it, Evelyn?"

Evelyn eyed Charlie with reproach. "Charlie, behave. It was not so long ago you appeared ruffled yourself after returning from a scavenger hunt."

"Ah, do not portray yourself so innocently, my sister. No one might have known of your trysts with Worthington. Even he failed to know. Nevertheless, you had them, and a swift trip to Gretna Green lay proof of yours." Charlie bit into a scone.

Evelyn smirked. "Yes, well, we did not pay a visit to discuss the secret encounters we shared with the gentlemen who are now our husbands. We are here to learn where Gemma's interests lie."

"Well, obviously with Lord Ralston. Even though Uncle Theo has forbidden Gemma to keep company with the rake," scolded Jacqueline.

"Which she has disobeyed," reprimanded Abigail.

"I only wish to know if he kisses as divinely, as smoldering as he appears." Charlie waggled her eyebrows.

"Yes." Gemma sighed through her muffled reply.

Abigail yanked the covers away, standing above her, waiting to hear the truth. She tried pulling them back, but Abigail fiercely held on, stripping them off the bed. Gemma rolled over, throwing a pillow over her head. However, they still wouldn't leave her in peace, throwing more badgering questions in her direction. When she realized they wouldn't leave, she dragged herself out of bed and curled into her favorite chair. Abigail handed her a mug of hot chocolate, and Gemma sipped at it, thinking of the excuses she would give them. However, there were none they would believe.

"Why are you not abiding by Uncle Theo's wishes?" asked Jacqueline kindly.

Gemma avoided their gazes. "My reasons are of a personal nature."

Gemma sipped from the cup and took a delicate bite out of a scone. When no one commented, she swept her gaze around to find all eyes upon her. She lowered her head and continued to eat her breakfast. After she drank her hot chocolate, she folded her hands in her lap, raised her head, and bestowed her family with a sweet, innocent smile.

"Personal nature, humph," muttered Abigail.

"If you wish to state your opinion, then do so, Abigail. But I am no longer going to share my secrets if you refuse to share yours," stated Gemma.

"I have no secrets," denied Abigail, sitting up straighter.

"So your decision to join the musical was because Jacqueline and I wore you down?" asked Gemma.

"Yes." Abigail played with the ribbons on her robe.

"Humph," muttered Gemma.

All attention swiveled to Abigail with this new bit of questioning.

Abigail glared at her, but Gemma held strong. There was a story behind Abigail's change of mind. Abigail had been adamant about not attending the musical until late afternoon when she rushed into Gemma's bedroom asking her opinion on which dress she should wear. Nor did Gemma miss Lucas's shock when Abigail joined them in the foyer before departing. She watched the display of emotions cross her cousin's face while they rode in the carriage. Lucas spent the entire evening with his gaze glued on Abigail, while Abigail ignored Lucas by conversing with the gentlemen Uncle Theo introduced her to.

"Your marriages must be dreadful if you still seek the comfort from these childish gatherings," scorned Selina Pemberton from the doorway.

"On the contrary, our marriages are more than pleasurable. You could only dream of the same for yours," purred Charlie. "Though, for that to occur, you must speak the actual vows, and it appears as if my cousin is dragging his feet. Does Lucas perhaps not wish to make you his bride?" Charlie tilted her head.

Selina gave a tight smile. "Quite the opposite. It is the reason for my visit. Colebourne sent notice to my father this morning to discuss the settlement, and Lucas invited me to join him for a morning ride. The duke will announce our wedding date soon. However, it is not soon enough. I fear the repercussions this family must take in stride for Abigail's appearance last night at the Mitchel Musical. I must comment on how disgraceful Lucas found her appearance. Throughout the evening I had to console him. He could not take his eyes off Abigail, and he feared which gentleman the duke introduced you to would strike your interest. In which I agree with him." Selina sniffed. "It will be foolish of you to fall in love with any of them. The embarrassment the family will suffer because of any infatuation on your part."

Gemma scowled. "Any gentleman would be so lucky to hold Abigail's attention."

Selina ignored Gemma's defense of Abigail and turned her spite onto Gemma. "And you, my dear," Selina snarled, "do not differ from your cousins. Sneaking away with a rakehell such as Lord Ralston. Have you no shame or respect for your family?"

Gemma glared at Selina. She wouldn't lower herself to Selina's level. She knew the venomous viper would spew her insults, and Gemma didn't have the arsenal to battle it. Nor did she care to. It wasn't in Gemma's nature to fight. If she responded, it would only give Selina more ammunition in her attack.

Abigail slipped her hand over Gemma's and squeezed in support. This was a gesture they had shared over the years whenever Selina slandered them.

"I hope you enjoy your ride with Lucas." Gemma smiled sweetly.

"Oh, I plan to. During the ride, I will do my best to convince Lucas of how your family should proceed with the season. Since our marriage grows closer, I am confident he will take my advice," gloated Selina.

"So, you still plan to marry the bloke?" drawled Duncan from behind Selina.

Gemma noticed how Selina paled once she heard Duncan. Duncan Forrester was Lucas's cousin on his mother's side and Aunt Susanna's son.

Duncan always ruffled Selina's feathers. However, Gemma sensed there might be more to the relationship.

Duncan leaned against the doorjamb and propped his feet opposite of him, blocking Selina's exit.

Selina recovered and turned. "There was never any doubt."

"Hmm, I thought otherwise," murmured Duncan.

Selina arched her eyebrow. "Then you, sir, were mistaken."

"No. I do not believe I am." Duncan pushed himself off the door and sauntered farther into the bedroom. He stopped before the tray of pastries and stuffed one into his mouth.

When he passed Selina, his arm brushed across hers, and Gemma saw Selina rub the spot softly from the contact. Selina's glare toward Duncan conflicted with the emotion sizzling in the air.

Gemma's head swiveled back and forth between the two, wondering the source of the tension between them. Was Gemma mistaken or did Duncan and Selina harbor feelings for one another? If so, it would complicate matters... Or would it? It could free Lucas from his obligation to Selina and make it possible for him to court Abigail. Oh, the possibilities.

Gemma relaxed in the chair, watching the drama unfold. Hopefully, it would draw the attention away from her.

Selina's fury grew the longer Duncan continued to ignore her. Duncan fed his face, oblivious to the storm brewing behind him. Or so Gemma thought. Duncan glanced at Gemma from the side and tilted his head slightly back, silently asking about Selina. Gemma gave a slight nod, and Duncan winked. Which brought forth a giggle from Gemma. A giggle she couldn't stop from erupting into laughter. Her amusement caused Selina to stomp her foot and let out a very unladylike growl before storming out of the bedroom.

It would appear Duncan held the magical ability to silence Selina's rants. Gemma wiped the tears from her eyes, catching her breath while Duncan raved about their breakfast spread.

"You ruined it, squirt," Duncan quipped.

"Did I? I thought Selina's visit ended most eloquently."

"But I aimed for more."

"More what?" asked Gemma.

Duncan winked. "More passion from the lass. After all, she hasn't seen me since the house party. I had hoped she missed me."

"The only person Selina Pemberton will ever miss is herself," retorted Charlie.

Duncan shook his head. "That is where you are still wrong, Charlie, my girl."

"And I thought you had laid all your craziness to rest." Charlie grabbed another pastry to eat.

"I never said I would."

"Tread carefully, my friend. Our uncle is on a mission and will not take kindly to your interference," warned Charlie.

"I disagree," said Duncan.

Charlie raised a brow. "How so?"

"Uncle Theo would not have invited me to join the family for the season if I were not to suit a purpose." Duncan strode confidently toward the door.

"Will one of you please explain what the two of you are blabbering about?" Jacqueline demanded.

Charlie tilted her head to Duncan, expecting him to explain.

Duncan flashed a sly smile. "Perhaps another time. I am late for the meeting with our great uncle now. However, it is wonderful to see you ladies again so soon. We shall enjoy the season together while I reside here during my stay. Until later."

After Duncan departed, all eyes centered on Charlie, waiting for her to explain the dynamics of Duncan and Selina. However, she would disappoint them. Charlie explained she wouldn't betray Duncan's trust. She'd made him a solemn vow to keep his secret. And everyone knew Charlie wouldn't budge, no matter how hard they tried. Charlie was a master secret holder. She betrayed no one who confided in her.

"Anyway, we did not gather here to discuss Duncan and Selina. We are here for Gemma." Charlie smiled mischievously.

Gemma knew when she was cornered. None of them would leave until she spilled her feelings. She might as well confess because her cousins were relentless, not to mention Abigail. But if she told them about Ralston, then she would make Abigail tell them why she had changed her mind yesterday.

"Very well. What is it you wish to learn?"

"Well, you already answered my question about his kisses. I thought he would be an excellent kisser. He has that devilish force about him. Not that I have any desire to discover for myself. I am perfectly pleased with Jasper's attention. More than pleased, actually," Charlie bragged.

The room groaned.

"Why are you risking Uncle Theo's wrath?" asked Jacqueline.

"I love him." Gemma smiled.

"Ralston?" squeaked Evelyn.

"Yes."

Evelyn nodded. She understood after suffering through the same quandary with Worthington.

"You cannot," said Jacqueline, shaking her head in denial.

"Why not?" asked Gemma.

Jacqueline held her hand up and ticked off the reasons behind her refusal. "The first reason is because Uncle has forbidden it. The second, he is not a suitable match if his scandalous exploits hold any truth. If you continue with this madness, you will only end up ruined. Lord Ralston is not the knight in shining armor you imagine he is."

"I only know what I feel, Jacqueline. My heart only wants Ralston and no other." Gemma placed her hands over her heart.

Jacqueline sighed. "I understand, dearest. However, I warn you that only heartache will befall you if you continue to make yourself available to Ralston."

"I disagree. You need to follow your heart as I did," urged Evelyn.

Charlie nodded. "I agree. You have my support too."

Jacqueline shot them both looks. "Neither of you should encourage her. Uncle Theo vetted Sinclair and Worthington for both of you, and you both fell into his trap. While your marriages are successful, that might not happen for Gemma. Ralston is not the gentleman chosen for her. It can only end in disaster."

"Who has Uncle chosen for me?" asked Gemma.

Jacqueline shrugged. "I have no clue. Only Uncle Theo knows. And perhaps Aunt Susanna."

Abigail, who had remained silent throughout the discussion, spoke up. "If Lord Ralston is the gentleman you wish to give your heart to, then I too offer my support. While I worry for your welfare if he does not return the gesture, I will not stand in the way for your chance at happiness."

Gemma smiled. With her family's support, they would make it possible for Gemma to have time with Ralston at every opportunity. She only needed one more person in the room to offer her support. Her eyes pleaded with Jacqueline to concede. Her smile grew wider the longer Jacqueline held out.

Jaqueline shook her head, finally giving in. "Very well. I offer my assistance too. Does Lord Ralston know what to expect from you?"

"I shall enjoy teaching him," quipped Gemma.

Jacqueline laughed. "I am sure you will."

"Now that I have confessed, Abigail needs to explain why she changed her mind." Gemma swung her head toward Abigail.

"There is no reason, Gemma," Abigail stressed. "I only wished not to remain home alone, that is all."

"Oh, Abigail. How insensitive we have been. While we have been enjoying ourselves, we have left you by yourself. Please accept our apologies," said Jacqueline.

Abigail reassured the room with her smile. "There is nothing to apologize for. I have enjoyed my time alone. It has given me time to reflect and make plans for my future."

"Which are?" Evelyn asked quietly.

"I plan to seek employment."

"There is no need. Uncle Theo has pledged a dowry for your future," argued Gemma.

"And I will be forever grateful for his generosity. However, 'tis not the path I wish to journey on." Abigail took a sip from her cup.

"But…" started Charlie.

"Please understand my needs. It was foolish of me to attend the musical. I only did so because my pride suffered an injury."

"Lucas," each girl muttered in exasperation.

Abigail's wistful smile saddened the other girls. Each of them wished for Lucas to see the creature before him, one who loved him with her entire soul. But his honesty and opinion on Abigail's standing only broke Abigail's heart into fragments, one piece at a time.

"All the more reason you owe yourself a chance to find happiness. Who says there is no gentleman worthy of you who exists in society? Please do not let our foolish cousin prevent you from discovering such a man. If at the end of the season you decide a different path, then we shall offer our support in fold. Please, consider Uncle Theo's offer," urged Jacqueline.

"Please, Abigail, for me," pleaded Gemma.

"Yes, show Lucas what he is missing by marrying Lady Dragon Snake," joked Charlie.

Evelyn shook her head, smiling at her twin's insult toward Selina. "Please, say you will enjoy the season."

Abigail stared at the ladies who always made her feel loved. Even though she was a servant's daughter, none of them had ever treated her as one. Ever since she came to live with the Duke of Colebourne, they had welcomed her as a member of their family. She cried along with them whenever they missed their parents. Laughed with them, most of the time at Lucas's expense. Shared with them the milestones of life. They were her family.

Abigail decided to agree to a season. She would spend time with them these next few months before she departed forever. For she couldn't endure watching Lucas create a life with Selina. Her heart couldn't suffer the agony. It suffered each day that grew closer to the event. Perhaps they were correct. Maybe there was another gentleman she might find contentment with. Someone who would take her far enough away and help her forget the love she held for Lucas Gray.

"All right. One season only."

The other ladies exclaimed with glee, jumping from their seats and pulling Abigail to her feet. They circled her in their familiar hug, laughing with excitement. Now that they had discovered Gemma's and Abigail's secrets, the other ladies intended to offer their support and aid when needed. Gemma's anticipation for the next ball would be hard to sustain.

She hoped Lord Ralston was as eager to see her as she was to see him.

Chapter Five

Ralston's eagerness to leave had nothing to do with the sudden appearance of Gemma Holbrooke. It had more to do with Lady Langdale. He didn't want the two to cross paths.

The widow had set her terms when he escorted her home after the musical. If he wanted to purchase the coin from her, then he must abstain from any contact with the lovely debutante. While Lady Langdale's words held no kindness, her message rang clear. Lady Langdale demanded his attention focused solely on her at the upcoming social events. If word spread of their involvement and she started receiving invitations again, then she would sell him the rare coin her husband had stolen. She was tired of the rumor mill slandering her for her reaction to Worthington's rejection. The widow tried to appear the victim to society, but the ton looked upon Worthington's countess and his adoration of his new bride with amusement.

Ralston didn't have a choice. His orders from Colebourne had been clear. He was to collect the coin no matter the cost. Even if it affected his pursuit of Gemma. It was only a minor setback, and Worth promised to help him with Gemma and the widow when needed.

Ralston knew he shouldn't pursue Gemma Holbrooke. But damned if the image of her eyes clouded with desire and her lips swollen from his kisses wasn't his downfall. Nothing else mattered when he held her in his arms.

Before long, his own father would intervene in this mess he had involved himself in. A mess his dear mother had created, but Ralston always took it on as his own to help keep her name clean. Once he finished Colebourne's final task, he would clear up his other fickle situation. After he cleared his debt, he could pursue Gemma, hopefully with Colebourne's permission.

In the meantime, he needed to keep Gemma and the widow apart. With the ballroom overcrowded, it shouldn't be too difficult for him to achieve.

Worth led Gemma off the dance floor and straight in his direction instead of returning Gemma to her chaperone. Her shy smile undid him, making him forget his promise to the widow. Ralston knew what hid behind the innocence she portrayed. A sweet girl who kissed like a vixen and had the power of bringing him to his very knees in a crowded ballroom to worship at her feet. They stopped before him, and Ralston only had eyes for Gemma. While he lost himself in the forest of her gaze, he forgot Worth stood at her side. He didn't care who saw the silly smile he directed toward Gemma.

"Ralston," Worth barked, drawing him from his haze of happiness.

"Lady Gemma, what an honor to be in your presence. Your loveliness this evening has captured me under your spell. Forgive me for my lack of a greeting." Ralston lifted Gemma's hand off Worth's arm and placed a kiss on her gloved knuckles. Her fingers trembled under his lips but calmed once he gently squeezed them.

"You, my lord, are an incorrigible flirt," teased Gemma.

"Only to you, my love."

"Ralston." This time, Worth growled a warning.

Ralston shifted his gaze toward Worth. "I only paid the lady a compliment."

"You know you did that and more."

Ralston shrugged.

"Do not make me regret your demand," said Worth.

"What demand?" asked Gemma.

Worth blew out his breath. "His demand to help the two of you with your clandestine courtship."

Gemma's eyes widened. "You wish to court me?"

"My wish with you is too indecent to speak aloud, especially in the company of one who is more prudish than I thought," drawled Ralston, nodding toward Worth.

Gemma blushed a becoming shade of pink. Ralston wondered if the blush covered her entire body and if so, how delicious she would look spread out on his bed with candlelight glowing around them. The longer he stared, the more her color darkened to the exquisite shade of a red rose.

"We are finished. This has been a mistake. One that I shall rectify by returning you to Lady Forrester this instant."

Before Ralston could stop him, Worth swung Gemma away and escorted her back to safety. She kept glancing over her shoulder at him. Ralston arched his eyebrow, indicating he meant exactly what he implied. She gave a slight nod, showing her pleasure at his comment. Ralston watched her thank Worth for the dance and converse with the party surrounding her chaperone. Her glance kept straying to him from time to time. Ralston knew it was risky, but he needed to find time alone with her this evening.

A hand gripped his shoulder, squeezing tightly. A head lowered to whisper in his ear a threat he shouldn't take lightly. "If you go near my niece, our deal is off," said Colebourne.

Ralston might have stiffened, but he wouldn't cower. "Which niece?"

Colebourne growled, moving in front of Ralston and blocking his view of Gemma. It didn't matter though. The image of Gemma was a permanent fixture in his soul. The duke no longer intimidated him as he once had. He was no longer a young pup of twenty. No, the past eight years had hardened him into the rake and scoundrel the ton believed him to be. All thanks to the man before him. And his mother, of course. But no longer. He would forge his own path soon. And his path contained Gemma Holbrooke, leading them on a journey of happiness.

"All of them."

"Well, considering you only have two who have not chosen a groom, it limits my options."

Colebourne narrowed his eyes. "I have three nieces still unwed and they will remain that way until I deem otherwise."

Ralston pursed his lips. "Three, you say. Do you have another niece hidden under a rock you have not paraded before the ton? One who perhaps brings shame on the family name? Who is this creature? I find I am intrigued, perhaps enough to disregard my feelings for the one I hold dear."

Ralston was baiting Colebourne, knowing who he regarded as his third niece. He wanted the duke to admit he considered Abigail Cason his niece, even though they shared no blood. It was the least the miss deserved for the humiliation Lucas Gray's fiancée attempted to throw at the poor girl at every turn. However, the duke wouldn't bite Ralston's lure. Instead, he abruptly changed the subject, throwing Ralston off.

"I heard you have been inquiring about the conditions of a few properties near Covent Garden. Now, why would the heir to a duke show any consideration toward vacant establishments? Especially when he hasn't a dime to his name. Do not think to double-cross me with the coin the widow holds," Colebourne pinned Ralston with his stare.

Ralston brushed an imaginary speck from his shoulder, not rising to Colebourne's bait. He had underestimated the duke by thinking Colebourne didn't watch his every move. When, in fact, he was under the deepest scrutiny of all. No matter, he wouldn't alter his plans. Instead, he would use them to throw Colebourne off his scent. If the duke thought Ralston might double-cross him, then the duke wouldn't focus so much attention on Gemma.

"If you will excuse me, Colebourne. I have promised Miss Cason the next dance." Ralston sauntered off, not waiting for the duke's reaction.

When Ralston neared Miss Cason, a young gentleman passed between them, carrying two cups of punch. The punch matched the gaudy blood-red decorations the hostess displayed throughout her ballroom. Ralston had steered clear of the drink once he noticed the guests' lips turned a bright red after drinking the dyed liquid.

Ralston watched the vindictive act as it played out before him, but couldn't offer a warning before the catastrophe struck. Miss Cason barreled into the gentleman, and he splashed the offending liquid down the front of her dress. The punch soaked into her once pristine white gown.

Gasps filled the air from the affront. One that she was innocent of, but to those who witnessed, her standing in society spoke otherwise. As Miss Cason tried to steady herself, her foot slipped on the mess. Ralston caught her before she tumbled to the ground, which would have caused her more embarrassment.

"I tried to warn you how Miss Cason's pedigree would shame your family. Why just look how ungraceful she is," Lady Selina remarked to Lord Gray.

More heads turned their way from those disparaging comments.

"Steady now. Hold your head high. Do not let anyone take away the power you hold," Ralston whispered.

"I hold no power, only humiliation." Abigail's voice trembled.

"No, you do not. Only if you allow them to make you feel that way. Now raise your head and smile. Oh, and do not forget to laugh at what I am saying. For I am quite humorous."

Miss Cason raised her head at his kind words, and he waggled his eyebrows to draw forth his commands. He squeezed her hands, and she smiled wide, her laughter at her mishap spilling from her lips. Ralston caught Gray's gaze over Miss Cason's shoulder and saw the gentleman struggle at not being the knight to rescue the damsel in distress. That alone brought satisfaction to Ralston, for it was the shrew standing next to Gray who had caused Miss Cason's distress. Let the bastard suffer for not protecting what he thought he held dear.

Ralston turned on his charm to help ease Miss Cason's discomfort by acting like a smitten suitor. "If I had known you were so eager for our dance, I would have arrived sooner."

Ralston meant his comment as a tease, but it mortified the young miss.

"I am so sorry, Lord Ralston," Abigail stuttered.

He patted her hand to reassure her. "No need. 'Tis not your fault."

Lady Forrester bustled behind Miss Cason, drawing her away from Ralston and seeing to Miss Cason's welfare. Gemma appeared on the other side of Miss Cason, offering comfort.

"I see you have someone to take care of you. I shall claim my dance at the next affair we both attend. In the meantime, it has been a pleasure to rescue you." Ralston lifted Miss Cason's hand and placed a kiss on her knuckles. His action led the guests regarding them like a sideshow to understand that he held no ill feelings toward her.

"Your actions are most kind, Lord Ralston. Thank you for helping Abigail," gushed Lady Forrester.

"No, no. You must let Gemma take my place, Aunt Susanna. We do not want to offend his lordship because of a silly accident," said Abigail, winking at Ralston.

Lady Forrester stood pondering, caught at a disadvantage. Ralston was aware of Colebourne's threat not to let Gemma anywhere near him. But if their family didn't offer to fill the dance he'd asked for, then it would look poorly on Miss Cason. Even though none of it had been her fault, the ton would judge the incident differently.

Lady Forrester's gaze flittered around the ballroom before answering. "Very well, if Lord Ralston is agreeable."

"It would be my honor." Ralston bowed before Gemma.

Abigail and Gemma laughed at his antics. Ralston smiled and offered his arm to Gemma, escorting her to the dance floor. Lady Forrester hustled Abigail away, with Lady Jaqueline following in their wake. Not far behind them, he saw Gray grab Lady Selina by the elbow and escort her across the room to her father. Then he turned on his heel and followed Lady Forrester and her charges.

Ralston made a quick sweep around the ballroom, taking note that the duke was nowhere nearby. This was his chance to steal Gemma away for a few moments. He positioned them near the open doors while the orchestra decided which music to play. At the first notes, the dancers started, but they misunderstood the direction and jostled together, causing many toes to be stepped upon.

Ralston acted on the disaster and made his move. He tugged Gemma outside, swept her down the stairs, and into the garden. The deeper they walked through the garden, the darker it turned. The only light guiding their path was the moon and the stars twinkling overhead.

He slowed his steps and stopped under a lamp near the fountain once he realized no one would disturb them. He twisted, twirling Gemma in a circle. Ralston wrapped his arms around her waist and dipped her low. At her gasp, he slowly drew her up into his arms. His conflicting thoughts gave him room for a pause.

Her dreamy expression and the softness of her lips beckoned him to kiss her. He fought against his desires. His act of luring Gemma into the darkened garden had been for one reason only, and that was to devour her lips and to behave as the scoundrel she believed him to be.

However, he wasn't that man.

Nor would he tarnish their future by pretending to be someone he wasn't. No matter how tempting he found her. If Gemma's only interest in him was because he was someone her uncle had forbidden her to see and she found pleasure in defying him, then he was not the gentleman for her. He wanted her to love him for his true self, not the man she thought he might be.

Gemma's heart raced with how close Ralston's lips were to hers. She hungered for his kiss. Why else had he lured her outside, if not for a tryst? The air sizzled around them with the unforbidden. Yet, Ralston hadn't tried to seduce her. When he pulled back slightly, disappointment settled over Gemma. Then he laced his fingers with hers and kept his other arm wrapped around her waist before he spun them in a circle. The first circle of many. He danced them around the fountain, humming a song near her ear.

The dance was one they could never perform in the company of others, with their bodies pressed tightly together and their steps slow, in tune with one another. His gaze held hers strongly, never once drifting away. If Gemma hadn't fallen in love with Ralston before, he now owned her heart. She didn't view him as others did. She saw him for the knight in shining honor he refused to allow anyone else to see.

Gemma didn't realize when their dance ended and Ralston stopped humming. They were hidden behind the fountain, in the darkest section of the garden. Their bodies clung to one another, and his desire pressed into her stomach. His grip tightened around her waist when she slid her tongue across her lips. Thirst for his kiss caused her to act wantonly.

"I ache to kiss your delectable lips. But I cannot." Ralston sighed, resting his forehead against hers.

"Why not?" Gemma whispered.

"Because I promised myself that I would not ruin you this evening."

"But have you not already done that very act?"

Ralston stared deep into Gemma's eyes. "How so?"

"You lured me away. We are alone, and you have me clutched in a possessive grip."

Ralston loosened his hold. "Am I hurting you?"

"No, my lord. I find it most comforting." Gemma pressed herself against him tighter. She lifted her hands and ran them along his lapels, smoothing them out. Her arms snaked around his neck and guided his head lower. She stood on her tiptoes, holding her lips but a breath away from his.

"Gemma," Ralston growled. "I am trying to act the gentleman."

"What if a gentleman is not what I desire? Perhaps I wish for you to act the scoundrel," she whispered.

"If that is how you perceive my character, then you are not the lady I viewed you as."

"That is where you assume wrong. I very much know who you are. However, I wish not to be the lady you think I should be." Her smile turned mischievous, and her eyebrows lifted. Gemma brushed her lips across his.

"Gemma," Ralston growled again.

"You may refuse to kiss me this evening. However, I shall not pass the temptation to feel your lips under mine."

Gemma pressed her lips to Ralston again, nipping along his bottom lip. Her tongue slid out and stroked back and forth, enticing him to open his mouth. When he sighed, Gemma slid her tongue inside and kissed Ralston with everything her heart desired.

The innocent strokes of her tongue undid him. The last of his resistance faded away. He could no longer deny himself the pleasure of Gemma. He took over the kiss, drawing out her sighs and capturing them into his soul. Gemma Holbrooke might present herself to the ton as an innocent miss, but she was really a siren beckoning him to her island.

Ralston's kiss shook Gemma to her core. Her body ached for his caresses, ached for him to make her his. She clung to him tighter and slid her hand through his dark strands, shivering with the anticipation of Ralston making love to her.

"Ralston," Gemma moaned.

"Barrett. My name is Barrett."

"Barrett," Gemma murmured into their kiss.

Chapter Six

Ralston backed Gemma toward the bench, but stopped once he heard his name and Gemma's whispered in the air. He should have never snuck her out of the ballroom. Now she risked ruination. At his hands, no less. He wasn't in the position to offer for her. Not yet, anyway. He had to secure the coin, and for him to do that, he must appear as a rake of the highest order.

If he were to convince Lady Langdale of his interest, then he couldn't have his name linked with Gemma's. Her cousin's recent marriage to Worth's brother, Reese Worthington, placed Gemma as the enemy. Worthington had tossed Lady Langdale aside when he married Evelyn Holbrooke. Lady Langdale had expected a marriage proposal from Worthington after he gained the title of earl. She had risked her reputation for three years as Worthington's mistress. When she learned of his marriage, she'd felt it the biggest betrayal and promised her revenge.

If anyone caught him with Gemma, it would destroy the mission. He would have to start from scratch to retrieve the coin from Lady Langdale.

"Where are they?" Ralston heard Evelyn Worthington asked near them. But because he and Gemma were hidden, he wasn't exactly sure where Lady Worthington was.

"I have no clue. I saw them headed in this direction," answered Worth.

"Then why did you not stop them?"

"I thought he would return Gemma before the dance ended."

"Well, he did not. And if she does not return soon, rumors will spread. So far, no one realizes she is missing. But her disappearance will not go unnoticed for long," hissed Evelyn.

Ralston pulled away from Gemma. He raised her hand to his lips and placed a kiss on her palm. "I am sorry, my love."

He tugged her with him to the front of the fountain where their searchers stood looking for them. Ralston squeezed Gemma's hand before releasing her and taking a step back. He cleared his throat, and the pair turned. Worth glared in frustration, and Lady Worthington rushed to Gemma's side, putting some much-needed distance between them.

"Are you mad?" Worth growled.

Ralston didn't answer. He only shrugged.

"Gemma, did Lord Ralston coerce you into the garden?" asked Evelyn.

Gemma laughed. "No."

Evelyn couldn't reprimand her cousin, not when, only a couple of months ago, she had put herself in the same position. Gemma had already professed her affection for the rake. And when no one noticed, Evelyn saw Ralston regard Gemma in the same manner. However, their courtship was as unorthodox as hers was with Reese. But the heart knows what the heart wants. And from where Evelyn stood, the longing she noticed in Ralston's gaze already declared the outcome of their union.

"He is not the mad one. I am afraid our family holds the rights to that affliction," declared Evelyn.

"How so?" asked Ralston.

Evelyn sighed. "Because I have decided to aid in your secret courtship."

Gemma squealed. "You will?"

Evelyn's lips thinned. "Yes. However, you must learn discretion. No more sneaking around at the entertainments you both attend."

"We promise," said Gemma.

"No," came Ralston's objection.

Gemma and Evelyn paused, looking at Ralston in surprise.

"There will be no courtship. Now or ever."

"I thought …" Gemma trailed away.

"You thought wrong, Lady Gemma. I am involved with another. I only lured you away to trifle with your affections, nothing more."

Both women gasped. Gemma paled at Ralston's cruelty. She didn't understand his change of behavior. One minute he was twirling them around under the stars, then holding her in his arms, kissing her senseless. Now he was denying it. She didn't believe him. Gemma didn't imagine how he made her float from his mere touch. Nor would he have reacted to her kiss if he felt differently.

"You bastard." Worth charged at Ralston, his arms swung out, ready to punch him.

Ralston ducked, then shoved Worth away. He straightened his sleeves and smoothed his coat back into place. He nodded at them before sauntering away.

Walking away was the hardest thing ever. But he had to because Lady Langdale hung back in the shadows, watching them. He didn't think anyone else had noticed the widow. He had to prove that he was toying with the girl's affection, aiding in her revenge.

When he paid Lady Langdale a visit after the ball, he would share in his joke on how he had lured Gemma Holbrooke to the garden to cause a scandal. This would help prove his allegiance against the Holbrookes. Once he convinced her of his loyalty, she would sell him the coin. Then he would plead for his forgiveness and court Gemma properly.

For now, he must stay true to his mission, no matter how much he enjoyed her seductive kisses.

Gemma watched Ralston walk away with a swagger to his step. She refused to allow her tears to fall because she didn't believe a word he spoke. She knew in her heart that he spoke false. Why? She held no clue. But she planned to discover the reason.

A hand touched her shoulder to offer comfort. She turned, and Evelyn's stare was filled with pity. "I am sorry. I misinterpreted Ralston's agenda."

"We both did," agreed Worth.

"No, you did not. Nor do I doubt him. He feels a need to keep our relationship secret, and it is for the best." Gemma smiled with confidence.

"How so?" asked Evelyn.

"Uncle Theo must not learn of our time spent alone. Ralston is aware of how Uncle Theo refuses a courtship between us. I imagine Ralston only said what he did so not to draw upon Uncle's wrath."

Worth looked at Gemma with pity. "You are wrong about Ralston."

Gemma only smiled at Worth. Then she linked her arms with his and Evelyn's to walk through the garden. She offered them no more. She would wait for Ralston to approach her again.

And he would. She had no doubt.

~~~~~

Selina followed the couple at a discreet distance. However, she wasn't the only one who trailed them. Lady Langdale kept to the shadows, pausing whenever she heard Selina's footsteps. To stay hidden, she had to duck behind a bush. When Lady Langdale stopped, it prevented Selina from getting any closer. She would have to circle around to catch the couple in a scandalous clutch.

Because she knew Gemma Holbrooke and Lord Ralston were having a secret rendezvous. Why else would they wander so far away from the ballroom? Selina had heard rumors of Lord Ralston's prowess with the ladies. This was perfect. If she caught Lord Ralston ruining Lady Gemma, then Papa could hold this over the Duke of Colebourne's head to threaten him with the need to secure a wedding date.

Selina feared the duke was attempting to break the betrothal. Selina hadn't wasted her formidable years for nothing. She planned to marry Lucas Gray and become the future Duchess of Colebourne by any way possible. Even if she must secure the ruination of the duke's ward.

There was no love lost there. At every opportunity, they snubbed their noses at Selina, never once inviting her to join them. When they finally issued an invitation, it was only to beat her at her own game. It hadn't been genuine.

Selina snuck through the bushes to find another location to spy on them. However, before she caught them in an inappropriate clutch, a most annoying pest interrupted her. It was the only way to describe Duncan Forrester. Any other phrase would betray the actual emotions she held for the gentleman… emotions she kept denying herself. To accept them would mean a scandal more damaging than the one she was trying to uncover this evening.

"Now what trouble are you up to?" whispered Forrester in Selina's ear.

A shiver ran along her spine. A shiver she stiffened her body against. She refused to allow the pleasure to consume her. It was troublesome enough when she lay in her bed every night trying to fall asleep.

"Why are you always following me?" Selina hissed.

Duncan raised an eyebrow. "I was not following you, my lady. I only came upon you while waiting for my latest conquest. In which, I must ask you to find another spot for your spying. I would not want to present the lady with the wrong impression."

"Lady? More like trollop," Selina muttered.

"Jealous?"

"Humph."

Jealous? Insanely. Duncan Forrester had been the very reason she had acted so spitefully against Abigail Cason earlier. Of course, Lucas Gray's attention toward the young miss didn't help any. Instead of focusing his attention on her, his fiancée, Gray gazed at Abigail. But was Selina jealous of the attention Gray paid Abigail? No. However, when she watched Forrester paying attention to every lady of the ton, jealousy rippled throughout her. Since his arrival in London, he had avoided her at all costs. Even when she threw herself in front of him, he never glanced her way. He would stroll by with no greeting, as if she were invisible.

It cut deeply. Selina never realized how much she craved Forrester's flirtations until he no longer teased her. Without them, it left her vulnerable, restless, and unsure of herself. Too many emotions she never cared for. But most of all, without his attention, she wasn't herself. Even after learning of his latest assignation, she felt like herself again. His attention made her feel cared for, even when he frustrated her.

Forrester wanted to chuckle at the indecision on Selina's face as she regarded him. He taunted her, hoping for any sign that she held an interest in him as he did her. When his uncle invited him to join the family for the season, he had jumped at the chance. He needed to leave Edinburgh because of a false accusation. His father agreed it was for the best to join his mother at Uncle Theo's residence. Apparently, Selina's father, the Duke of Norbury, had pressed his uncle to make a date for the wedding by the end of the season. Which only left Forrester a few months to secure Selina for himself.

Most would call him crazy for wanting this woman. His family found it humorous to call themselves mad. Why should he be any different?

Forrester pushed past Selina, peering between the bushes to see what drew her attention. It had to be something worthwhile. Why else would she risk her reputation by slinking through the darkness alone? What drew his eye only meant one thing for his family. Scandal. Lord Ralston had Gemma clutched in a scandalous embrace, leaving no thought to where their intentions lay. It would appear he needed to rescue another cousin. He turned back around to Selina. He would sacrifice himself for his family with much pleasure.

"So will you take your leave? Or perhaps you wish to join us?" Forrester's smile turned wicked.

"Why have you returned to London with your insufferable manners?"

"Why, to win your affections and steal you away from my cousin."

Selina narrowed her gaze. "And engaging in secret trysts with your lovers will somehow win my affections?"

Forrester shrugged. "I need something to keep me occupied in the meantime. Until you realize you cannot live without me."

"That day will never come. Now move out of my way." Selina tried to shove him away. However, she held no strength to move him an inch. She pounded her frustration on his chest. At every opportunity, he thwarted her plans to ruin the Holbrooke chits. First with Charlotte and Lord Sinclair, now with Gemma. How could she gather information to hold over their family and secure her marriage to Gray without ruining one of them?

Voices drifted closer, and Selina panicked. If anyone caught her alone with Duncan Forrester in a dark garden, it would be her ruination for everyone to witness. She strained her ears, listening in tense silence. When the voices took to another direction, Selina breathed a sigh of relief. Forrester had swept her behind him to hide her identity. He kept his arm wrapped around her waist and held her against his back.

"Unhand me, you barbarian," Selina hissed.

"Shh, love. We are not in the clear yet."

His threat seemed to quiet Selina. However, it caused him panic. He heard footsteps coming from different directions. If he didn't act swiftly, someone would catch them and assume they had planned to meet. When the steps grew nearer, Duncan did the only thing he could. He turned, pushed Selina farther into the darkness to protect her, and pressed her against a tree. Lowering his head, he captured her gasp with a kiss.

Not just any kiss. He wanted to let Lady Selina understand the threat behind his kisses. Before the season ended, she would be his.

He ran his tongue over her lips, coaxing them open. Soon her gasp turned into a sigh. Forrester stroked his tongue along hers, teasing her with a passion they could share. When she melted into his arms, he took the kiss deeper, wrapping his arms tighter around her. Before he caressed her soft skin, someone slipped through the bushes a few steps away from him.

A throat cleared. "Um, so sorry for the interruption."

Forrester Duncan looked over his shoulder. "No bother, Ralston. Just sampling the wares for later this evening."

Ralston laughed. "Pleasurable?"

"Best I have ever tasted."

Ralston smirked. "Word of warning, Forrester, if your lady is unmarried, take caution on returning her to the ballroom. The garden is full of creatures. Some are cuddly, the others are vipers."

Forrester nodded at Ralston before the chap sauntered away. Before he returned his attention to Selina, he noticed Graham Worthington escorting Gemma and Evelyn back to the ballroom. With the coast clear, he must deny his passion and make a safe return for Selina. Now more than ever. Her absence would go noticed before too much longer. Selina's father might neglect her, but he was always aware of her whereabouts.

When he faced Selina, she held a look of terror upon her face. "I am ruined," she whispered.

"No, love. Ralston did not see who you were." He tucked a stray curl behind her ear.

Selina's eyes widened. "He knows. He will tell."

"No, Ralston is honorable. And he did not see the lady I kissed. I kept you hidden."

Selina shook her head. "No, no, no."

Forrester pulled her tight, holding her and whispering words to quiet her fears. Once she relaxed in his hold, he held her away, urging the need for them to return. While he enjoyed this side of Selina, he needed her normal personality to shine through at this moment. He needed her cold and calculating and knew just how to make that happen.

"Since I have ruined your reputation, shall we continue?" Forrester whispered, nuzzling her neck.

He slid his hand down and grabbed her derriere, pushing himself into her, then started inching her dress higher to stroke her silken thighs. Selina froze in his embrace and gasped. Her hands came between them and shoved him backward. Once she put distance between them, her hand struck him across the face.

He dropped his arms, stepped back, and gave her his wickedest of smiles. "I shall take that as a no. Such a shame, your sighs awaken my desires when we kiss. I suppose I must slake those desires with the lady who is soon to arrive for our scheduled rendezvous."

Selina growled and stomped away, heading back inside. Duncan followed close by in case he had to pull her into the shadows. When she reached the maze opening, she glanced back over her shoulder. He stood where she could see him and blew her a kiss. When she glared at him, he laughed loudly enough to reach her. She shook her head in annoyance before disappearing. Forrester chuckled some more. He loved ruffling her feathers.

He only hoped he preoccupied Selina's thoughts long enough for her to forget Gemma and Ralston. Forrester needed to warn Gemma and give her a lecture. Ralston was out of Gemma's league. She didn't need to involve herself with a rake whose only intention was to break her heart.

~~~~~~

Once they reached the ballroom, Gemma pretended to laugh at something Worth said. She squeezed his and Evelyn's arms for them to join in with her laughter. She gave the other guests the picture of three family members enjoying each other's company. When the guests realized there was no gossip to learn, their glances slid away, and they returned to their conversations. Soon their path led them to Aunt Susanna and Abigail.

Worth peeled his arm away and bowed to them. "I found pleasure in our conversation, Lady Gemma. Thank you for accompanying us, Evelyn. Enjoy the rest of your evening."

"Thank you for our walk. I enjoyed myself, Mr. Worthington."

Worth nodded before strolling away.

Gemma turned her attention to Abigail and inquired about her wellbeing. Aunt Susanna's intense stare settled over her. She prayed her aunt wouldn't question her whereabouts. However, her luck wouldn't fall in her favor.

"Mr. Worthington is quite the dashing fellow. He may not be a lord, but his brother is an earl, no less. I will confer with your uncle on a match. Would that please you, Gemma?" Aunt Susanna inquired.

Gemma cringed. Since Worth had helped rescue her from a scandal, she hated to use him to her advantage. But she couldn't let Aunt Susanna learn who held her heart. If she spoke of her interest in Worth, Uncle Theo might support the match. Then that would allow Worth to court her. Worth and Ralston were the best of mates, so she only had to convince Worth to aid her and Ralston into spending time alone. Gemma hoped her newfound friendship with Worth would endear him to help.

Gemma's face lit up with the offer. "Yes, it would. Will Uncle Theo agree? I shall suffer disappointment if he does not."

Aunt Susanna patted Gemma's hand. Then her lips lifted into a devious smile for a brief second before turning into a caring one. If Gemma didn't know any better, she might have thought Aunt Susanna had sprung a trap. "You just leave your Uncle Theo to me. By tomorrow afternoon, your uncle will grant Mr. Worthington the offer of winning your hand."

After her promise, Aunt Susanna left the girls to themselves. Since Evelyn had married Lord Worthington, her standing presented them with a chaperone nearby. Soon, Charlie and Jacqueline joined their small group.

"Where were you?" Jacqueline hissed.

"Ralston led Gemma deep into the maze and hid them behind a fountain. If it were not for Graham, Gemma's standing as an innocent debutante would be shattered," explained Evelyn.

Charlie laughed, and Abigail shook her head in disappointment. However, Gemma didn't care. She had danced in Ralston's arms this evening. And not the proper dance of lords and ladies. No, their dance was one for lovers. She smiled, remembering how she'd stolen a kiss from him this time. She'd caught him unaware, and it heightened the intensity of their attraction.

"I know that dreamy expression. If you are thinking of Lord Ralston, then why did you agree to Aunt Susanna's offer with Mr. Worthington?" asked Abigail.

"To throw Uncle Theo off the scent. Brilliant idea!" Charlie nodded, smiling.

Jacqueline shook her head this time. "You are foolish if you believe Aunt Susanna fell for your interest in Mr. Worthington."

Gemma shrugged. "She seemed sincere."

"Only for you to fall into her trap. She helps Uncle Theo with his mad matchmaking. Did you not learn from Charlie and Evelyn's debacles? She plants the idea. Uncle Theo sets the plan. Then you fall into their trap as an unassuming victim. You may hold overwhelming emotions for Lord Ralston, but if you are not careful, you will find yourself betrothed to Mr. Worthington. Especially since Evelyn has proven to Uncle Theo how worthy the Worthingtons are."

Gemma waved her hand at Jacqueline. "Pshh. You speak nonsense."

"Oh well, let it be known I warned you." Jacqueline pinched her lips.

Gemma looked at her family one by one and noticed they stood behind Jacqueline's words. A small part of her knew Jacqueline spoke the truth. Her uncle was a devious man who manipulated others into what he desired. However, she always twisted him around her little finger. And this would be no different. She would play the demure debutante, pretending an interest in Worth's courtship while she secretly pursued Lord Ralston until they could be together. But first, she must get Ralston to admit the reasons for his duplicity.

Only then could they have a future.

Chapter Seven

Ralston waited in Colebourne's study for the duke to return home. He'd received the summons before he left the ball. This left him unable to pay attendance on Lady Langdale. Worth had warned him about the lady's temper. On the morrow, he feared he would learn the full effect of his absence.

Ralston heard the animated chatter of the duke's wards in the hallway. He wished to stick his head out of the study and make himself noticed. But that would only annoy the duke. Ralston walked a fine line after leading Gemma away for a secret tryst. He hoped it wasn't the reasoning behind his summons. Had Colebourne learned of his earlier behavior?

He grimaced, running his finger under his cravat. The garment now seemed too tight. He started pacing in front of the lit fireplace, contemplating an excuse over his scandalous behavior. He also prepared an offer for Gemma's hand. Even though it was his true intention, he wanted to secure his freedom first.

"What has you so nervous, Lord Ralston?" Colebourne asked.

Ralston paused. He'd not heard the duke enter the study. His thoughts scrambled on how to respond. He stood waiting for the duke to address him further. Colebourne narrowed his gaze, raked him from head to toe, then continued to his desk. The duke lowered himself in the chair and lifted the lid to the cigar case. He motioned for Ralston to take one, but Ralston shook his head, refusing the offer. He detested the vice.

"What is the news? Have you made progress with the widow?"

"Yes. I believe I am earning her trust."

Colebourne lit the cigar. "Mmm. I am under a different impression after this evening's ball."

"How so?" Ralston walked closer to the desk, drawing his arms behind his back. He balled his hands into fists. However, he kept his stance relaxed. Ralston had years of practice. After all, his own father was a duke who demanded respect. Ralston had learned at a young age not to cower to an authority figure.

"It appeared you fell out of favor with Lady Langdale in the ballroom. However, my sources informed me you fell back into her good graces after you paired with her in a card game. What is your next move?"

He tightened his fists. "My move had been to accept her invitation to accompany her home after the ball. However, your summons prompted me to decline her invitation."

"How did she react?"

"I explained the urgency of my father's request with a family matter, and she understood. She extended her invitation for tomorrow evening instead."

Colebourne arched an eyebrow. "In which you plan to accept?"

"You leave me no choice, Your Grace," Ralston gritted out between his teeth.

Colebourne took a long draw from his cigar. "No. I have not. I want this business cleared up within a week. Do you think you can seduce Lady Langdale to accept your offer for the coin in that allowed timeframe?"

"Is there any doubt?" Ralston scoffed.

"Your cockiness is showing, Lord Ralston."

Ralston shrugged. Lady Langdale would accept his offer by tomorrow, but he wouldn't let the duke know that. Let Colebourne stew awhile. He planned to drag this mission out longer. He didn't understand the rush to retrieve the coin, but he would use the next week to discover why. Then he would inform the duke of his possession of the coin and request permission to court Gemma. If the duke refused, then the coin would go to the next highest bidder. Ralston already had out feelers on who else might be interested in the treasure. He planned to hold this over Colebourne's head. The coin for the girl. It was more than a fair exchange.

"We are finished."

Ralston wanted to growl at the duke's dismissal. Colebourne focused his attention on a stack of papers on his desk, Ralston already forgotten.

Before he made it to the door, it opened to admit Lady Forrester. "I am sorry, Colebourne. I did not realize you had company. Good evening once again, Lord Ralston."

Ralston bowed slightly. "Lady Forrester, always a pleasure. I bid you a good evening."

He took himself off, closing the door behind him. As he walked along the hallway to the entrance, he noticed the servants' absence. Darkness shrouded the house. Then he recalled Lady Forrester had carried a candle with her inside the study.

He paused at the front door, glancing back along the hallway. The door stayed closed to the duke's study. Ralston looked up the stairs, then back to the study again. Upstairs lay his true heart's desire. He started up the steps, his tread stealthy. Ralston would take the risk to hold Gemma in his arms once more tonight.

He knew which bedchamber was hers. In his line of work, it was his duty to learn the layout of a peer's residence and who slept in each room. The duke may think he watched his every movement, but it was Ralston who employed people to learn every aspect of the duke's life. The duke, like others, thought Ralston was a rake who gambled, whored, and drank in excessive amounts. It was an image that had taken him a lifetime to create, one he'd crafted to make believable and would use to his advantage tonight… And every night until he captured the damsel he most desired.

~~~~~

"Why would you meet with Ralston at such a late hour?" asked Susanna.

"Why else?" A mischievous smile lit the duke's face.

"You are aware he lured Gemma into the garden under the pretense of dancing?"

"Yes, I am quite aware of what happened this evening. Please peek outside and see if our guest has taken his leave." Colebourne waved his hand toward the door.

Susanna opened the door in the briefest of cracks and watched the marquess stroll along the hallway. When he turned, she snuffed out her candle. It took her eyes a minute to adjust, but she saw him pause near the foot of the steps, contemplating if he should leave. After a few more glances back and forth, the young lord made his decision. He prowled up the stairs, keeping his steps light, and stayed pressed against the shadows.

She turned and smiled at her brother-in-law.　　"He has not."

"Excellent. His action explains my very reason for summoning him here this evening."

Susanna released a weary sigh. Colebourne played with fire, allowing these gentlemen to ruin his charges. He ran the risk of one of the gentlemen refusing to make an offer of marriage. Ralston was a risky candidate. His prowess amongst the ladies of the ton was well-known. Not to mention the rumors of his nefarious exploits were always on the tip of the gossipers' tongues. Tonight only proved how maddening Colebourne's matchmaking attempts were.

"If word gets out …"

"It will not. Rest easy, Susanna. With two successful matches under my belt, settling the rest of the girls shall be easy."

Susanna rested in a chair. "Evelyn and Mr. Worthington returned Gemma to my care after her extended absence. When I questioned her on the character of Mr. Worthington, she expressed an interest. Now why would she do that if her interest truly lies with Lord Ralston?"

Colebourne chuckled. "Ahh, she is sneaky. Sneakier than her cousins. She hoped to throw us off. What did you tell her?"

"That I will plead Mr. Worthington's case with you."

Colebourne nodded thoughtfully. "And so you have. I want you to extend an invitation for Mr. Worthington to join our family in our box at the theatre in three nights' time. I have it on worthy authority that Lord Ralston has agreed to escort Lady Langdale to the play. Between now and then I will drop in the gossipers' ears of a budding romance between Gemma and Mr. Worthington."

Susanna shook her head. "Are you trying to cause a scandal?"

Colebourne tapped the ash from his cigar into a tray. "No. I only wish for Ralston to hurry and finish the task I assigned him to. I need to secure Gemma's hand. Norbury is applying pressure for me to make an announcement soon. I need to get Gemma settled, so I can move on to Jacqueline. Then I will clean up the mess I created by betrothing Lucas to Lady Selina. To do so, I need all the girls wed or the scandal of Lucas and

Selina will render it impossible to secure the girls' hands. I made a promise to see to their welfare, not for them to have scandal tarnishing their reputations."

She narrowed her eyes. "Hence my issuing an invitation to have Duncan join us for the season?"

"Yes."

"Perhaps I do not agree with your plans."

Colebourne chuckled. "But you do. Do you not?"

Susanna sighed. "Yes."

"Then we shall proceed with Gemma for now. Do not worry, my dear, I will secure Duncan's future."

"By schemes."

"No. By matchmaking." Colebourne winked at Susanna, laughing at how his mad plans were coming together so smoothly.

Chapter Eight

Ralston crept along the hallway. When he rounded the corner to Gemma's bedroom, he halted. A door creaked opened. His heart lurching, he pressed against the wall, praying to go unnoticed. He relaxed when Gemma appeared in a button-down robe. Her hair was unbound, falling in waves along her back.

Ralston watched her slowly close the door. When the click of the doorknob entered its slot, her body tensed. She stood still. When no one checked on the noise, she relaxed. Ralston chuckled. Before she noticed him, he came upon her, wrapping one arm around her waist and settling another gently against her mouth.

He lowered his head to whisper in her ear. "Are you going somewhere, love?"

Gemma gasped against his hand. He turned her around in his embrace. When she opened her mouth to speak, he placed his finger on her lips to keep her quiet. Then he opened her door again, ushering them inside. He leaned against the door, pulling Gemma closer. She sighed against his chest.

Ralston tipped Gemma's head up. "Are you going to answer my question?"

"I overheard the maids discussing your appearance in Uncle Theo's study. I feared he learned of our time in the garden."

"Were you on your way to defend my unscrupulous behavior?" Ralston teased.

"If need be, I will."

Ralston stared at her lips, thirsty for a drink of her sweet nectar. "There is no need, my love. My meeting with your uncle was only business. Nothing more."

"What kind of business? Is it the same reason why you brushed me aside earlier?"

"I cannot discuss the business I conduct with your uncle at this time. Please forgive my insensitive behavior earlier this evening."

Gemma tugged at his cravat. "I will only forgive you if you explain why you behaved so cold once Evelyn and Worth came upon us."

Ralston sighed, pulling away and walking around the room. At the window, he drew the curtain aside and peered into the garden. He weighed his options on how to appease Gemma. He planned on telling her the truth once he completed his assignment. The risk ran too high for her to understand his motives. Especially with Lady Langdale on the warpath against her family. Gemma may portray herself as sweet and innocent, but he noticed the backbone and determination in her gaze when she pursued what she wanted. He thanked his lucky stars her choice was him. He only had to keep secrets from her for one more week.

When he turned, the sight before him stunned him. Gemma had lit a candle and discarded her robe. Ralston gulped. She stood in the candlelight in a soft pink gown. An innocent garment with thin straps and a row of buttons that tempted him to rip them apart. She may have appeared confident, but Ralston saw how her body quivered under his stare.

"Ahh, love. You tempt the very devil."

Gemma took one step after another until she reached him near the window. The moonlight shimmered through the sheer curtains, highlighting Gemma's womanly curves. When she reached him, she slid her hands up his chest until they circled his neck.

"I have no wish to tempt the devil. Only you, Barrett."

Ralston tried to follow the conversation, but her husky voice purring his name made him lose all rational thought. Not to mention her fingers sliding along his neck and through his hair.

"What if I am one and the same?"

"Are you?"

"I could very well be," Ralston muttered before claiming Gemma's lips under his.

And he was the devil for entering her bedchamber in the dead of night and ravishing her lips with one sinful kiss after another.

He inhaled her sweetness into his deplorable self, proving he was the devil for taking her soul into his and never relinquishing his hold. Gemma was the opposite of the women he usually pursued. He'd known the moment he laid eyes on her that she would be his downfall. Everything he had worked for these last few years, he risked losing with each pull of her lips against his.

But the greedy devil he was, he would risk his life for any token of affection she threw his way.

He backed Gemma toward the bed. When her legs hit the mattress, Ralston lowered her down and followed. He held himself above her and watched her chest rise and fall with anticipation. He trailed his hand up her arm to her shoulder and back down again. This time, when he swept his hand upward, he slid the thin strap down.

"Do you know how desperate I am to tear this gown off you?" he whispered before sliding the strap back up and securing it in place. He bent his head, placing a soft kiss on her shoulder. Her pale skin glistened under the candlelight.

Gemma stared at him with her eyes wide, pleading for him to caress her. Coming upstairs to her bedchamber had been a mistake. A grave mistake if he were to get caught. He didn't want to ruin Gemma. But if he didn't leave soon, he couldn't stop himself.

"Order me to leave, Gemma," he pleaded.

Gemma shook her head. She couldn't tell him to leave when she craved his body pressed against her. She wanted to experience every wicked act he'd whispered in her ear at the Mitchel Musical. Her body trembled under his touch. Not from fear, but from the whispers of his scandalous promises.

Gemma slid her hand to his cravat, loosening the tight knot. "I will not," she whispered.

Ralston lowered his head to Gemma's forehead. He closed his eyes, fighting with himself. For the first time ever, he needed to draw forth enough strength to act like the gentleman he truly was. However, with Gemma lying underneath him, she was too much of a temptation to resist.

He'd stop after he sampled one kiss.

When Gemma shifted underneath him, her leg rose along his, and he lost any resistance he clung to. Ralston devoured Gemma's lips, drawing each kiss into a sensual longing that would be his demise. Once Gemma realized his resistance had slipped away, her hands went wild on his body, tugging at his clothing. He grabbed her hands and lifted them above her head, clasping her wrists.

He shook his head at her. "No, my love," he whispered.

He slipped the delicate strap off her shoulder and tugged the gown lower to reveal her heaving breasts. His hand lowered, filling his palm with one globe of perfection. A perfect match. He brushed his thumb across her nipple, and it tightened into a hard bud.

"Barrett," Gemma whimpered.

Barrett stroked his tongue across the bit of cherry. Sweet. He tugged it between his lips, sucking softly on the delectable fruit. They were sweeter than he had imagined. Gemma squirmed under his hold, which only heightened Barrett's pleasure. His palm held her breast to his mouth while he feasted on her. While his mouth pleasured her, his tongue stroked their passion higher. His lips nibbled where his teeth scraped across the sensitive bud. He savored the sweet temptation.

He switched his hands to lower the other side of her gown. When the globes glistened in the candlelight, he moaned. He bent his head, gifting the other breast with his devotion, while his free hand slid Gemma's gown up the leg she had wrapped around his waist. Barrett spread her leg opened wider and caressed the inside of her thigh.

Soon her whimpers turned into sighs. His fingers brushed across her curls. He only wanted one touch of the wetness clinging to them. Then he would stop. Only one caress…

One caress turned into multiple caresses. One stroke of his finger soon turned to two. Until Gemma writhed underneath him, demanding more. The longer he pleasured her, the wetter she became. Her need throbbed against his fingers when he slid them inside her wetness. Perhaps a kiss or two would appease their desires.

"Barrett," Gemma pleaded.

Barrett lifted his head and watched Gemma come undone under his touch. Her back arched off the bed, and her nipples tightened into hard cherries. She pressed her core into his hand, and her hands thrashed around, trying to break his bond. The wildness in her eyes drew Barrett under her spell. He was powerless to the passion she wrapped them in. His need to worship at her feet was stronger than his need to act like a proper gentleman.

Hell, he'd lost that resistance when he climbed the steps to her bedchamber. Why deny himself what he desired the most? And at this moment, it was the sweet flavor of Gemma on his lips. Maybe then he could stop this madness before it went any further.

Swiftly, he released her wrists and sank to his knees, pulling her hips to the edge of the bed. He bent his head, inhaling her sweet scent. Sin. Sweet sin. The most inviting fragrance to sinful decadence.

"Barrett?"

"Shh, love. I cannot resist."

"I do not wish for you to," Gemma whispered.

Barrett raised his head to see Gemma's lips curve into a seductive smile. He growled and lowered his head for his tongue to strike out and soar a path across her wetness. When Gemma moaned and pressed herself into his mouth, he lost his battle and let the madness take over. He needed more than a kiss or two to ease the ache in his body. He devoured the sweet treat, drawing Gemma's pleasure higher. His fingers stroked in and out while his tongue followed. He licked and sucked, feeding the greedy hunger inside him.

Gemma closed her eyes, lost in the pleasure Barrett strummed from her body. She arched into his mouth, making demands only he could fulfill. She never imagined she would find such pleasure in this act. One time, while in a bookstore, she had found a copy of prints displaying sexual scenes. She remembered blushing, but never looked away while she flipped from one page to the next. Gemma never imagined gentlemen and ladies performing such scandalous acts. They didn't repulse her, only intrigued her.

Barrett fulfilled every fantasy with the first brush of his tongue against her.

Her body molded to his touch, arching and bending to his will. She didn't understand why he kissed her one moment, then tried to resist her the next. Nor did she care at this point as long as he continued to dominate her senses with his attention.

Barrett's mouth left her a quivering mess. She prayed he never stopped. His strokes grew bolder, and Gemma surrendered to his passion with wild abandonment. Her desire grew out of bounds, demanding Barrett to ease the ache that consumed her.

Gemma's body thrashed under his domination. He knew the exact moment when he controlled her desire. Passion swirled around them, swaying to the exotic dance of pleasure. That he thought a mere nibble would appease him only proved what a fool he was. No, he wouldn't find satisfaction until his cock was settled between her heavenly thighs, and he slid into the warmth his mouth now devoured. He grew harder imagining her sweet cunny clutching him and throbbing around his cock. He ached to savor her sweetness when she came undone on his tongue, but he couldn't wait.

Ralston needed Gemma now.

Barrett rose and backed away from the bed, his fingers undoing the placket of his trousers. When the air swept over his exposed skin, he froze. The full implication of what he set to do hovered on his conscience. There would be no return if he took Gemma's virginity now. He loved her, but the duke would refuse his offer on the morrow, leaving Gemma vulnerable to whatever the duke decided for her. However, once he finished the duke's orders and presented himself to the duke as the gentleman who loved his niece, the man would surely not disapprove of the match. Gemma marrying a duke's heir would be the ultimate coup for his family.

Gemma watched Barrett wrestle with his decision. She refused to let him leave without loving her in full. To tempt him to finish what he started, she stood up, a mere breath away from him, and slid her nightgown off her body to pool around her feet. Then her hands reached out to undo Barrett's shirt, her fingers quickly working on the buttons as if she were a skilled courtesan. No, she wasn't one of those. Only an eager woman hopelessly in love, one who ached to have her true love make love to her.

Gemma lifted his shirt over his head and ran her fingers across his firm chest, dipping over his rippled abdomen. She smiled. Barrett was divine. Gemma stepped closer and placed her lips on his chest, trailing soft kisses toward a path of danger.

Gemma lowered herself with the trail of her kisses. Her hands brushed his aside at his trousers and she finished unbuttoning him. Before she could continue, Barrett growled and lifted her in his arms. His mouth ravished her with a need for her to fulfill. Gemma wrapped her arms around his neck and pressed her breasts against his naked chest. The sensation scorched her senses, and Barrett swallowed her gasp in his possessive kiss.

He laid her on the bed and stripped out of his trousers. Gemma held her arms open for him to join her. He settled above her, his cock pressing against her wetness. Gemma trembled with eagerness at becoming Barrett's lover.

"This is your last chance. Tell me to leave. Now, Gemma, while I still hold on to a brief amount of honor," growled Ralston.

"I will never tell you to leave."

"You will one day."

"Never," she whispered.

Gemma slid her legs up and wrapped them around Barrett's waist, leaving him no doubt of what she desired most. He growled and pressed his hips against hers. All it took was a stroke of her tongue along his and Barrett slowly slid inside her. It wasn't enough. Gemma wanted all of him. She raised her hips and pressed against him, pushing him deeper inside. She froze at the tight invasion.

Barrett paused when Gemma froze, calling himself a bastard. Her eagerness prevented him from easing her pain. She raised her panicked eyes to his. Before he slid inside Gemma any deeper, he palmed her breast, teasing her nipple. He bent his head to draw the dark cherry bud into his mouth, teasing until Gemma softened in his arms once again. When she sighed, he slid inside a little deeper. He raised his head to see her look of panic had changed to desire.

But her body wasn't ready to accept his full length. So he continued his amorous seduction until Gemma melted into a pool of unchecked passion. As he lowered his hand and played with her bud, her wetness slid between his fingers. With each flick to her clit, his body slid in deeper and deeper until Gemma accepted him fully. He never broke eye contact, guiding their bodies in a slow dance by sliding in farther with each stroke.

Gemma felt like she could die at any second. The pain she'd experienced when Barrett first slid inside her had disappeared into a searing sensation of fulfillment. So pleasurable she thought she would perish from it. Her body ached with a need Barrett fulfilled with each stroke. Gemma climbed higher and higher to a destination out of her reach. She clung to him and soon moved in sync with him, heightening her pleasure even more. She closed her eyes and lost herself in the ecstasy of their passion.

"Open your eyes, love. I want to stare into them while we soar to heaven."

Gemma opened her eyes to Barrett's intense stare. His eyes were filled with every emotion running through her. When he lowered his head to take her lips in a sweet, gentle kiss, Gemma unraveled. Barrett moaned in her kiss, pressing himself deeper. They came undone, soaring for the skies as they clung to one another. When Gemma fell from soaring, Barrett caught her and held her close to his heart. Nothing in her life had impacted her so deeply before.

"Is it always so remarkable?" Gemma whispered in awe.

"If so, I have never indulged in the sensual act before you."

"Never?"

"Never, my love." He placed a soft kiss on her lips.

Gemma sighed. Warmth invaded her soul every time he called her "my love." She didn't want to ruin the moment by questioning him about his previous lovers. His reputation amongst the ton preceded itself, and her own family had warned her away from the rake. However, it no longer mattered. That was the past, and their future stood before them now. She only wanted to lie in the splendid aftermath of them becoming one. A more blissful feeling, there was none.

Barrett spoke the truth to Gemma's inquiry. Never had he became one with a lover before. When they made love, it was as if it were his first time. No other encounter had been so fulfilling and profound.

She lay content in his embrace, drifting to sleep. He turned them on their sides to stare at Gemma. A smile rested on her face, while her eyelids twitched with her dreams. He wanted to spend a lifetime gazing upon her. He wished he could awaken with her in his arms, but that wish would have to wait before it became true. Now, he must depart before someone walked in on them.

He reluctantly pulled himself out of their embrace and dressed. He couldn't leave the same way he entered. No. He would take the risk and escape through the secret passageways. Barrett had learned of the duke's fixation on them when looking at the designs for his many homes. He chuckled. The duke would be furious to learn why Barrett held such knowledge about him.

It was the duke's own fault. He should have never dangled Gemma in front of him, then denied him the very treasure he wanted. He continued to hold threats over Barrett's head to prevent him from pursuing his obsession. The duke would soon learn that those threats were meaningless. The only thing he treasured lay but a few feet away, nestled in her bed. More than his reputation and definitely more than his mother's.

With one last glance, Barrett hit the secret latch, and the mirror swung open. He slipped through the opening and closed it behind him. He kept to the sides of the walls and treaded softly in case anyone else was wandering the hallways.

When he reached the bottom, he slipped outside and swiftly strode through the gardens to the alleyway by the stables. After he reached a safe distance, he slowed his walk. He was no longer in any danger of being caught. With a whistle to each step, Barrett continued to his club. He wanted to learn of any gossip from the ball he attended earlier this evening.

The Duke of Colebourne smoked his cigar, staring out at the gardens from his bedroom window. After blowing out a puff of smoke, a devious smile overtook his face. He shook his head at the latest gentleman who thought he'd outwitted him regarding his ward. When would they ever learn they were no match for him?

Colebourne breathed a sigh of relief that he had moved the date of Ralston's mission forward. The bloke was in too deep and had no clue. His niece Gemma charmed the very devil and drew him into her web. Ralston never stood a chance. The duke chuckled before retiring for the evening.

Tomorrow promised to be another eventful day, one he must remain on his toes for.

Chapter Nine

Gemma waited in the parlor for Worth to join them. His sisters had arrived with Evelyn for afternoon tea. Noel had whispered to her that Gemma's uncle had summoned Worth for a visit. Noel had voiced her worries, but Gemma assured her it was because she told Aunt Susanna of her interest in Worth, which led to her uncle to grant his permission for their courtship.

"Why ever would you do that? I thought your interests lie with Lord Ralston," asked Noel.

A dreamy expression overtook Gemma as she thought of where her interests lay with Lord Ralston. A scandalous interest involving many sinful pleasures. Gemma sighed, remembering Barrett's kiss. The stroke of his body inside hers. His whispers of sin. A warmth stole over her from the heat of the blush spreading across her body.

"I see." Noel giggled.

"Is it more than obvious?" whispered Gemma.

"Only to a trusted friend who you confided in. However, said friend is in dire need of details to keep the confidence strong."

"Very well. But you must swear what I am about to confess remains a secret. You must not tell another soul."

"I promise." Noel twisted a pretend lock on her lips.

Gemma glanced about the room, making sure she had enough privacy for her confession. Lady Worthington walked into the room, announcing she had decided to join them after all since Worth had to call on the duke. Noel's mother and Aunt Susanna soon bent with their heads together to scheme. The other ladies gathered around Abigail, offering their opinions on the gentlemen who had called upon Abigail earlier in the day. Instead of the ton shunning Abigail because of the accident at the ball, the complete opposite occurred. Gentleman upon gentleman had called upon Abigail today. Their appearance sent Lucas stalking away in a jealous rage. Gemma learned Lord Ralston had confessed to several gentlemen at his club about his disappointment with losing out on his dance with Miss Cason and how he hoped to engage the young miss in a dance at the next ball.

Her true love really was a knight in shining armor. He'd rescued her best friend, nay her sister by heart, with a simple gesture to elevate Abigail's standing in society. It warmed her heart and endeared Barrett to a lifetime of kisses. She couldn't wait to thank him properly, in the way a paramour might thank her lover.

Gemma told Noel about their dance in the garden and how Ralston's actions affected her, then how he'd abandoned her to Worth and Evelyn. Then she explained how she'd given Aunt Susanna the idea for Worth to court her. Gemma confided her doubts on why Ralston kept pulling away from her, but held confidence that he wanted to court her. But her uncle remained an obstacle. She embellished the garden scene to explain why a blush had washed over her. Gemma kept Barrett's lovemaking to herself. While she wished to confide more in her friend, she also didn't want to. What she shared with Barrett was only for them to cherish.

"Oh, my, how romantic. You are a lucky lady, my friend." Noel sighed.

"Yes, I believe I am. Now we need to find you someone as amazing as my Barrett."

Noel arched a brow. "Barrett?"

"Mmm, yes." A dreamy expression washed over Gemma's face.

"Gemma, please be careful. I would hate for the duke to marry you off to another gentleman."

"Nonsense. Uncle Theo would never dare."

"I am afraid he will. I overheard Evelyn and Reese discussing how your uncle will prevent any union between Lord Ralston and you. You must be careful," Noel warned her friend.

"I intend to. Hence the reason for showing interest in Worth. If my uncle believes I've given my regard to another, he will forget about Barrett. Which leaves any stolen moments we share secure from his knowledge."

Noel bit her lip, hesitating. "While I am head over heels happy for you, I believe you are too confident."

"Pssh." Gemma waved Noel's words away.

Noel pinned her with a stare. "Do not say I did not warn you. From what I have learned, your uncle is extremely devious in his matchmaking attempts. You are no exception."

Gemma tapped her finger against her chin. "Yes, I see what you mean. Uncle Theo has a way to undermine someone, leaving them believing it was their idea when all along it was his. However, I have had many years to learn his deviations. I am confident that within a weeks' time, Barrett and I will confess our love and Uncle Theo will consent."

"I hope you are correct. Just promise me my brother will not suffer from a broken heart."

Gemma squeezed Noel's hand. "I promise I shall not hurt Worth."

"What is this promise you are making?" Worth stood over them, catching the ladies unaware that the gentlemen of the family had joined them.

Gemma smiled at him. "Why, I am promising Noel that I will not break your heart this season."

"Perhaps you already have," he teased.

"Have I, Mr. Worthington?" Gemma's smile turned mischievous.

Worth clutched his heart. "Broke it. Tore it in two. Walked upon it with your indifference. All the while I have been your adoring slave waiting for any sign of affection."

"In which I have shown you my undying devotion, granting you but spare moments of my time. Are those seconds not long enough for you?" Gemma's eyes twinkled.

"I must find comfort in what you offer, my queen." Worth bowed before Gemma.

Noel rose, shaking her head at their tomfoolery. "Oh, brother. I cannot endure anymore."

Gemma watched Noel join the others and smiled at Worth. When she had first met him, she had put her desire for Lord Ralston on hold to explore her feelings for Worth. But they didn't compare. She felt only friendship toward him and nothing more. He was a fabulous flirt and lifted her ego, 'twas all. She patted the seat next to her. Once he sat, he twisted to the side to regard her.

Gemma waited patiently under his intense stare, knowing he had much to inform her. When he still didn't speak, she tried to prompt him. "Well …?"

Worth shrugged and settled more comfortably against the cushions. His intention was clearly for her to confess why her uncle had demanded a call today. Gemma cringed, knowing her false statement from the evening before would be her demise. She hoped it didn't cause any ripples in their friendship.

She rolled her eyes. "Very well, I shall begin. After our walk last night, I might have given the false impression to Aunt Susanna that I was interested in a courtship between us."

Worth laughed. "Oh, that is what I love about you. Your ability to sweeten the interactions of our meetings, even down to your infatuation with me. I do not know if I should feel honored or declared a fool. What do you think, my dear?"

Gemma winced. "All right, you have made your point, Mr. Worthington. Shall I plead for your forgiveness or plead for assistance?"

He pretended to think. "Mmm. I think I shall enjoy both."

Gemma rolled her eyes. "You are an insufferable male."

"Ahh, but one that you enjoy as a friend. Do you not?" Worth tilted his head.

"Yes. Are you terribly upset?"

"No, but a warning in advance should not be too much to ask for."

Gemma's smile brightened. "I promise you shall have one. However, in my defense, I did not know they would strike so soon."

Worth gave her a pointed look. "Gemma, do not be so naïve. Your uncle's primary goal this season is to see his wards wed. The season has already started, and he has three wards and a son still to settle. That leaves no margin to make unnecessary connections."

"So what did my uncle require of you?"

Worth's lips tightened, remembering the duke's orders. "He invited me to join your family at the theatre this week. Once I accepted the invitation, the duke granted me his permission to pay court to you. More like he insisted, leaving me no room to deny his request."

"This is perfect."

Worth frowned. "How so?"

"You can provide cover and we can give Uncle Theo the impression that we are falling in love. In the meantime, you can help Lord Ralston and I spend time together."

"I thought this smelled of Ralston. Luckily, you escaped getting caught in his clutches last night. Ralston may be a friend, but he is trouble. Whatever notions you have regarding him, you need to forget them and find someone else to focus your devotion on. But not me. While you are lovely and I enjoy the time spent in your company, I am afraid I only consider you a friend," Worth emphasized.

Gemma shook her head. "Forgetting Lord Ralston is no longer an option, I fear. I love him too deeply. I only need your help for a few more days."

Worth sighed. "This not only affects you. If I court you, my mother will get the impression that I care for you. If you think Colebourne is relentless in finding you a groom to settle with, it is nothing compared to the lengths my mother will go to secure me a bride. Not to mention Reese forbade me to trifle with you."

Gemma smirked, already having come up with an answer. "But that could only be to your advantage. If we can convince your mother of our union, then she won't try to set you up with her friends' daughters. I saw her at work the other evening at the Calderwood Ball. You had to dance the whole evening with every lady she threw in your direction. Noel and I had quite a joyful evening watching your distress."

Worth snorted. "You are a conniving minx."

Gemma laughed. "Do you not see my point? She will no longer focus on trying to see you settle if she believes you are serious over another lady. We have already left our families wondering if our flirtations are sincere."

Worth listened to Gemma's points. They only hammered home the need to enter this fiasco. However, if he pretended an interest in Gemma, then it would keep his other activities hidden. He already walked a fine line with Reese regarding his frivolous pursuits. Only, this would infuriate his brother. Reese had been adamant that Gemma Holbrooke was off-limits. But then, he always enjoyed upsetting Reese. Also, Gemma made a point regarding his mother. Ever since she arrived in town, she kept trying to set him up.

The only flaw in her plan was his own feelings for Gemma. They were a mixture of friendship, thrown in with a hint of desire. Gemma was a lovely lady, full of life and spice. She twisted a man's emotions into a state of confusion. At times, they fell into friendly conversations. Then when she was most vulnerable, he wanted to hold her in his embrace and kiss a smile on her lips. However, he never crossed that line.

Which led him to believe the connection they shared wasn't strong enough for forever. Especially after he'd witnessed her with Ralston. Ralston was Gemma's soul mate. And as a friend to both, it was his job to bring them together before Ralston screwed up the opportunity at his feet. With one wrong decision, it could all go up in smoke.

"All right."

"You agree?"

He nodded. "Yes."

Gemma bounced on the seat and grabbed his hand. "You will not regret this."

Lady Selina smirked. "How sweet. However, if I were you, Mr. Worthington, I would beware of Lady Gemma's enthusiasm."

"How so?" asked Worth.

Selina gave her a knowing smile. "Why, she shares her favors freely with another."

Gemma tried to pull her hand from Worth, but he held firm. He wouldn't allow this viper to strike at his friend. "I am sure you have mistaken Gemma for another lady."

Selina's smile widened. "No. I know what I saw when I followed her and Lord Ralston into the garden last night."

"You are mistaken because Lady Gemma and I took a stroll in the garden, accompanied by her cousin and my sister-in-law, Evelyn." Worth shrugged. "Lord Ralston must have enticed another lady who shared a similar appearance to Gemma in the gardens for his sinful pleasures."

Selina shook her head. "No. I am not mistaken, Mr. Worthington. I intend to inform the duke of what I witnessed. His wards are bringing disgrace upon my family with their improper virtues."

Duncan spoke from behind Selina, surprising the group. "My cousins with improper virtues? I say not. Now, I know of another young lass who holds those characteristics. Tasted her myself last night. Mmm, would love to experience another sample of her. Perhaps it was I who you came upon last night in the gardens. I can vouch for Gemma being in Worth and Evelyn's company. I saw them myself in the garden, with no Ralston in sight. Hell, that bloke had his hands full with Lady Langdale all evening."

Gemma watched Selina transform when Duncan appeared. She tried to hang on to her spiteful control, but a shiver shook her frame when Duncan mentioned his tryst with another lady. Was it Selina? If so, their encounter rocked the very foundation of Gemma's family. She didn't mistake the longing in Selina's eyes before her frustration took over.

Selina turned and snarled, "Why must you interfere in every conversation I seek?"

Duncan shrugged mildly. "If they were only innocent conversations, I would not. However, when you strike out with your vengeance at those I love, I cannot stand by and allow your spitefulness."

"You are an interfering barbarian," hissed Selina.

"Now you ... Well, you hold knowledge of my feelings for you without me burning any ears," Duncan drawled.

Selina gasped. "You would not?"

"Keep pushing me, lass. I very well might."

Selina paled before scurrying away to the safety of Lucas standing alone near the windows.

"May I have a word alone with Gemma?" Forrester asked Worth.

Worth nodded. "Yes. Thank you for coming to Gemma's defense. Lady Selina strikes fear wherever she goes. I have never met such a frightening lady before."

Forrester's eyes flashed in anger. "You do not know her as I do. You will refrain from forming an opinion that would degrade Lady Selina in anyone's eyes."

Gemma rose too, needing to settle peace. Worth looked at Gemma in confusion. Gemma shrugged.

"I shall call on you later this week for a carriage ride. I will bring Noel along as a chaperone." He lifted her hand and placed a kiss across her knuckles.

"Thank you. I look forward to our time together."

Once Worth walked away, she faced Duncan and watched him as he kept his gaze focused on Selina and Lucas. He shook his head when Lucas put distance between them.

Gemma's thoughts on Selina grew conflicted as she noticed the sadness lingering in Selina's gaze. Throughout the years, Selina had been a thorn in their sides. This was a trait she had shown no one. Perhaps they had treated Selina too harshly in the past. Gemma's eyes drifted back and forth from Duncan to Selina, and she realized that at least one member of her family held the lady in high regard. However, it was the wrong gentleman.

"You wished a word?" asked Gemma.

Duncan swung his gaze toward her. "Yes. You need to be aware that if you continue to sneak around with Ralston, someone will catch you. I prevented Selina from seeing the tender embrace you shared with Ralston. However, I have since learned that it was not your first time alone with him. If you are not careful, Uncle Theo will discover your affections for the rake and your fate will not be what you most desire."

Gemma nodded. "Thank you for your advice. I will take better precautions in the future."

"Why Ralston? The man is a rake who spends every indiscretion under a different skirt. Why tarnish your reputation with the likes of him?"

Gemma narrowed her gaze. "How exactly did you prevent Selina from spying on me?"

"That is none of your concern. I did what I had to, to guard our family's honor," Forrester gritted between his teeth.

"Was it a most terrible sacrifice?" she whispered.

"Yes, most terrible." Forrester kept his voice dull and steady.

Gemma smirked. "Hmm, I thought so."

"No, you do not. Nor will I explain. Only know that I do not approve and I will not stand by and let Ralston ruin you," he threatened.

Gemma leaned in. "Perhaps you are too late," she whispered before walking away to join the other ladies.

Gemma settled on the couch next to Abigail and smiled at leaving one person in her family dumbfounded. She had grown weary of listening to how Lord Ralston wasn't the gentleman for her. How dare they? Her heart knew what it most desired. Did they not realize she no longer cared for their opinions? She only wanted their acceptance, and she would set out to prove to them how worthy Barrett was for her.

Chapter Ten

Selina sat at a small desk in the parlor she used for writing her correspondence. At least her father and servants thought she did. Yet, none of them ever asked to deliver them. Like all the other times, she was penning a letter she would never send. This letter would find the same demise, licked away by the flames of the fire.

Selina wrote an apology to Abigail Cason. In it, she confessed why she had acted so vindictively. Then she explained to Abigail of her longings, confessing her deepest desires as if she wrote to a dear friend. Selina sighed, wondering how that would feel. To actually have a friend she could confide her deepest secrets to. But Selina lashed out towards Abigail and any other lady before they could hurt her instead.

She had never been reprimanded for her behavior. Many referred to her as a shrew, a viper, and other derogatory terms one called an enemy. For the most part, it never bothered her. Until recently. The one gentleman Selina didn't want for an enemy had grown furious at her antics. Their future didn't bode well if he continued to keep a negative opinion of her. It was an opinion Selina strived to change.

"Lady Selina, you have a visitor."

Selina didn't know whose expression showed more disbelief, hers or the servant's. No one ever paid her a visit. Selina stuffed the papers in the drawer and rose to sit on the couch. She ordered the butler to show her visitor in and to have tea and cake served. Selina didn't inquire as to who her visitor might be. She held too much excitement over someone calling on her. She hoped it was Lucas Gray, but the butler wouldn't have shown Lucas to the parlor with Selina alone. Perhaps it was one of his cousins, wanting to include her in their circle before she married Lucas.

However, disappointment settled over her when the butler showed Lady Langdale into the parlor. Selina refused to rise from her seat for the lowly lady and signaled the servant to cancel her request for refreshments. She held no clue why this woman called on her, nor did she care. The lady wouldn't be staying long enough to feel welcome.

"Lady Langdale, this is a surprise."

The lady glanced around the room before answering her. Greediness lit the baroness's eyes as she took in everything. "I expected your parlor filled with silly debutantes. But then, you do not bother with simpleminded misses, do you?"

Selina offered no explanation for her empty parlor. A parlor that always sat empty and always would. Even after she married Lucas, nothing would change. Only a more depressing sense of loneliness.

"Is there a reason for your visit?" Selina's voice turned haughtier.

"I had hoped to form an alliance."

"How so?"

"May I?" Lady Langdale swept her hand at a chair.

Selina nodded. Lady Langdale sat down and pulled off her gloves, making herself comfortable. As much as Selina wished to remind the widow of her station, her curiosity won out. "Please explain yourself. I do not wish to explain your presence to my father."

"No, that would be most difficult, considering the circumstances," Lady Langdale baited.

Selina quirked a brow. "And those would be?"

"All in due time. Perhaps you could offer me some refreshments."

Selina sighed in annoyance. "No, I will not. I wish for you to make your point and take your leave as soon as possible. Now, what is it you wish to discuss?"

"Are you aware of the affair I carried on with Lord Worthington for three years before his marriage? One that I held out hope for a wedding proposal."

"No."

"Now I plan to begin an affair with Lord Ralston."

Selina shook her head in confusion. "Why would your past and present lovers matter to me?"

"Because they involve the Holbrooke chits. Evelyn Holbrooke ruined my chance at becoming Lady Worthington, and now Gemma Holbrooke stands in my way with Lord Ralston." Lady Langdale sneered. "The gentleman is infatuated with the chit. I cannot hold his attention when he finds avenues to dally with her."

Selina stared at her blankly. "I do not understand how I can assist with your problem."

Lady Langdale arched an eyebrow. "Do you not?"

Selina sat on guard. She wasn't a simpleminded miss and could par with the best of them. However, Lady Langdale had her at a disadvantage. "No."

"It is quite simple. Rumor has it that you dislike the Holbrooke ladies and they return the sentiment. I witnessed your distaste for Colebourne's ward, Miss Cason. A most brilliant display by shoving her into the gentleman passing by with the punch. After all, she deserved it for taking away the attention your betrothed seemed to pay toward her instead of you. Then there is the matter of your own betrothal put on hold until your fiancé's cousins walk down the marriage aisle. Which does not seem fair to me." Lady Langdale offered Selina an understanding smile.

"What are you suggesting?" Selina asked carefully.

"I want Lord Ralston for myself, and I will not share him with Gemma Holbrooke. One Holbrooke chit stole my chance at moving up the steps of society. I will not allow another to prevent me from what is mine. I only need you to whisper in Colebourne's ear of Lady Gemma's indiscretions."

Selina frowned. "But will that not secure Lady Gemma and Lord Ralston to a marriage?"

Lady Langdale laughed. "No, my dear. For it will not be Lord Ralston's name you whisper, but Mr. Worthington's instead."

Selina gave Lady Langdale a questioning stare. "Now you have me confused."

"I learned this morning that Colebourne has given Mr. Worthington permission to court Lady Gemma."

Selina scoffed. "Then spreading rumors of them seems silly."

"Not so." Lady Langdale raised an eyebrow. "I overheard Lord Ralston asking Mr. Worthington to pretend interest in Lady Gemma to throw Colebourne off his scent."

Selina leaned forward. "So, you want me to falsely inform her family to trap Lady Gemma and Mr. Worthington into marriage. Then not only will you have your revenge against the Holbrookes, but you will also have your revenge toward Lord Worthington too. Since you cannot have him, you will make a member of his family marry someone they do not want."

Lady Langdale nodded. "Exactly. I thought I would have to draw you a picture. You appeared most dense for a while."

Selina bristled under the lady's words. How dare this lowly peer talk to her so? She was on the verge of ordering her from the parlor, but she wanted to learn more of Lady Langdale's plans. Selina didn't plan to agree. She only wanted to determine how the lady planned to extract her revenge. Selina took enjoyment from the Holbrookes' trials.

"When do you plan to entrap them?" asked Selina.

"Starting tomorrow evening. I heard a rumor that Colebourne invited Mr. Worthington to join his family at the theatre, and I convinced Lord Ralston to invite me to share his box. Now I need you to attend and follow Gemma once she sneaks away from her family. Through my observations this season, I have noticed she takes any opportunity she can to find herself alone with Ralston."

"I am sorry, but I will not aid you in your revenge. I have my reputation to preserve, and I cannot allow myself to become entangled with someone of your standing." Selina sat back in her seat.

"I see." Lady Langdale pinched her lips.

"Good. Now if I can please ask you to take your leave."

Lady Langdale wagged her finger at Selina. "Ahh, I told you that I understood, not that I would accept your refusal, Lady Selina."

Selina gritted her teeth, tired of their tedious conversation. "You must because you cannot change my mind."

"Very well. Then I guess I shall just have to wait for your father to join us."

Selina laughed. "My father will not listen to a word from your lips."

"Oh, I believe he will. Once he hears how his daughter spends her evenings in dark gardens with someone other than her intended." Lady Langdale smiled smugly.

Selina paled at the comment. She didn't think the lady had seen her at the Kanfold Ball. If she had, then had she also witnessed her time alone with Forrester? She must, or she wouldn't sit so confidently, waiting for an agreement to help her ruin Gemma Holbrooke.

When Selina remained quiet, the baroness continued. "I noticed you following me last night, hoping to witness the very scene I hoped to see. Mr. Worthington and Lady Worthington ruined my chance to catch Lady Gemma in Ralston's arms. However, imagine my surprise to find another debutante clutched in a rake's embrace. One that was not her intended." Lady Langdale gave her a devious smile. "I must say, it was a steamy clutch. I can see how you were not immune. Duncan Forrester is quite the gentleman with a reputation. He can warm my bed any night of the week. Has he warmed yours yet? If not, I imagine it will be soon after what I saw. It is a tricky situation for you. Is he not Lord Gray's cousin? Family gatherings must be entertaining."

Selina swallowed hard. "I was never in the gardens. You have mistaken me for another foolish girl who fell in that devil's arms. I am offended that you would even suggest such an incident."

Lady Langdale held up a palm. "Oh, please stop the melodrama with your pretend infuriation. I know what I saw. If you do not agree to help me, then I will give the ton proof of your indiscretion."

Selina stiffened. "You have none."

"Do I not?" Lady Langdale pulled out a torn piece of fabric from her reticule.

Selina wanted to moan in dismay. She'd noticed her torn gown when she arrived home and her maid commented on it. She'd offered an excuse of tripping during a dance and how her heel caught on the gown, ripping it apart. Her maid tsked the shame of ruining the beautiful dress and offered to repair it. Selina declined and gifted the maid with the gown, extracting a promise for her not to inform the duke. Selina feared her father wouldn't allow her to buy any more gowns if she kept ruining them.

"'Tis what happens when a lover takes you passionately against a tree," Lady Langdale said matter-of-factly. "Or the bushes. Or against a door. Quite anywhere, really."

"Fine," growled Selina.

"Excellent." Lady Langdale smiled brightly now that she had gotten her way. "We shall begin tomorrow. Drop a few comments here and there to leave the duke wondering. Then by the end of the week, you will have convinced the duke to force Lady Gemma and Mr. Worthington into a marriage neither of them wants. Then I will seek my ultimate revenge on them."

"Your revenge? I do not understand."

"There is nothing for you to understand, only orders for you to follow. Are we in agreement?"

Selina nodded. "Yes."

Lady Langdale rose and departed the room, leaving Selina confused. Not only confused, but now fearful that the lady held the power to ruin the dynasty Selina had hoped to create with her marriage to Lucas Gray. That dynasty was now crumbling around Selina, all because she couldn't resist Duncan Forrester's kisses. Kisses that awakened a part of Selina she never even knew existed. Kisses she must forget because they weren't her destiny.

She must stay on her toes around Lady Langdale. She could play the lady false and inform her of Gemma and Ralston's trysts until she learned more. Perhaps even befriend the lady, spewing her hatred of Lucas's family and earn Lady Langdale's trust. Then when it became time, she would go to Forrester and persuade him to help her. After all, Lady Langdale's threats affected him too.

Chapter Eleven

It had been three days since he'd seen Gemma, and every one of them was longer and lonelier than the day before.

Sure, he'd spent them filled with visits to his club, wooing Lady Langdale, and scheming with Worth. However, none of those activities compared to holding Gemma in his arms and ravishing her lips. Not to mention her delectable body. After having a taste, he craved her with a need unclear to himself.

The few times he'd caught sight of her, she had always been out of his reach. A temptation dangled before him, teasing him from what others had forbidden him to touch. Her family guarded her virtue as if it were still innocent. He knew no one had learned of his time in her bedchamber. What enflamed his desires the most were the secretive smiles she bestowed on him when she thought no one looked.

He scowled as he watched her family in their private box. Graham Worthington sat at Gemma's side, playing the consummate gentleman, flirting with her. Ralston curled his hands into fists. He had hoped the rumors were false. However, the sight before him proved otherwise. Over the course of their meetings this week, Worth had never once mentioned his courtship of Gemma. Instead, he'd discovered the deception in the betting books at White's. There were a variety of other bets placed on Worthington and Gemma's courtship. Everything from their first kiss to the proposal to the actual wedding itself.

When he settled into his own box, Ralston made eye contact with Gemma. Guilt racked her gaze. At her expression, it felt liked she punched him in the gut. It took his breath away. He never took his gaze off her, and she refused to glance his way again. Instead, she treated him to her enjoyment of having Worth as a companion. The traitors. Did she seek revenge because he made love to her and never offered for her hand? Was this her way of securing a groom in case her uncle learned of her lost innocence?

Either way, he deserved an explanation, one he would take before the evening ended.

For now, he needed to focus on his assignment and not on the tempting blonde who unraveled his sanity with each of her throaty chuckles. Instead, he planned to charm Lady Langdale when she arrived. Ralston walked a fine line on ruining any attempt to gain the coin Colebourne demanded. However, after learning some recent information this afternoon, he would secure his offer with the lovely widow.

At least his parents wouldn't join them in the box this evening. His father had left town to visit the ducal estate, and his mother had remained at home to spend time with his sisters. He should pay them a visit this week. He missed their silly faces.

Lady Langdale swept into the box with a dramatic flair. A hush fell over the theatre when he stood up to greet her and usher her into a seat. He waved a hand for the servant to open the bottle of champagne. Ralston had set the scene, creating a sense of seduction for the widow. He needed her to believe he wanted to be her next protector. By showing the ton his intentions, with the extravagance of his wealth on full display, he wanted everyone to whisper tomorrow of what they saw. For they wouldn't gossip on the actors' performances, but on how Lady Langdale had snagged herself a marquess. A marquess who would one day become a duke. Ralston needed Lady Langdale assured of her position before he sprung his trap.

Ralston lifted the widow's hand and placed a kiss on her glove. She laughed at his attempt to seduce her and made a show of the champagne served, letting the other spectators know of their abundance. Her vulgar show of his wealth set Ralston on edge. The widow thought she had him cornered with her demands, but he only played a part. A part that would be her demise.

He only hoped Gemma didn't believe what she saw. If so, he needed to remedy that. He hoped to secure himself a moment of her time this evening. He'd written a letter that explained the reasons for his absence. Perhaps Worth would give the letter to Gemma. But could he still trust his friend?

The lights flashed, prompting the theatregoers into silence. Once the play began, Ralston raked his gaze across the crowd. Every eye remained fastened on his box, waiting for the next scene, and he wouldn't disappoint them. He leaned into Lady Langdale, whispering seductive words in her ear. From time to time he would brush a kiss across her cheek, along her neck, and on her bare shoulder. The widow presented herself as an experienced woman who held the skills to please a man. However, the blush spreading down her throat proved she was no match for him. He wanted to chuckle at how easy it was to seduce her.

He paused in his seduction when his gaze clashed with Gemma's. Ralston noticed her lips tremble under her pinched expression. The heartache in her stare stabbed him in the chest. However, he couldn't stop. Their future depended on his betrayal. He tried to plead his apology with his stare, but she turned away, concentrating on the stage. Ralston closed his eyes to refocus the strength he needed to continue with this farce.

At the intermission, Lady Langdale's acquaintances flooded his box. His fury grew when they shoved him to the back. It was then that he saw Gemma leave her box, with Worth following on her heels. Since the widow didn't seem to care if he were present, he could find Gemma. He tore out of the box and ran down the hallway, shoving patrons away in his attempt to catch Gemma.

~~~~~

Gemma couldn't endure much more. With each whisper and caress Ralston gave Lady Langdale, her heart ripped further apart. When he pressed his lips to the widow, Gemma thought she would go mad. She didn't understand the drama unfolding before her. She only wished for it to disappear.

When Ralston hadn't attempted to see her since they made love, Gemma had made excuses for his absence. She didn't want to believe he'd trifled with her for his amusement and that she was only another debutante he'd ruined in a long line of others. No. What they shared was two souls joining as one. He must have a very reasonable explanation on why he was trifling with another lady. Either way, she could no longer keep watching him.

She rose to get away, but Worth stilled her with his hand on her arm, urging her to stay seated. Gemma tried to shake him off, but his grip stayed firm. Gemma lowered herself long enough for him to believe she had listened to his silent advice. It wasn't long before she was saved from a lecture. The curtains closed for intermission, and everyone rose from their seats to stretch their legs. Gemma rose again.

"Gemma, please do not..." Worth pleaded.

"I must."

Gemma fled and rounded the corner toward Ralston's box. She looked over her shoulder and spied Abigail following her with Worth not far behind. Thankfully, the hallways were full, and no one had seen her without an escort. Before she reached Ralston's box, a set of arms grabbed her from behind and bustled her along an empty corridor.

Panic ran through her, and she fought her attacker by scratching at his hands. When he thrust her into a storage closet, Gemma opened her mouth to scream for help.

Warm lips descended on hers, softly coaxing her mouth to open. Gemma's panic disappeared on a moan. Only one man held the power to affect her so. Ralston. Gemma's turbulent emotions exploded, and she clung to him, demanding him to soothe her battered soul. Her mouth opened and her tongue stroked alongside his, entangling in a ferocious need of surrender. When their kiss slowed, Gemma pulled away to draw a deep breath. Then she shoved herself away, taking a step back into the tight area.

Ralston stepped forward, but Gemma held a hand up for him to stop. She couldn't express her anger if he were to come any closer. He already took the very breath from her soul. While their kiss proved how powerful their passion was for each other, she wanted answers.

"Why?" Her voice hitched.

Ralston gave her a desperate look. "I can explain, love. However, time is not in our favor. You need to return to the crowd before the hallways empty."

Gemma shook her head. "I cannot bear to return to my seat and watch you paw at Lady Langdale."

Ralston sighed. "It pains me as much as it does you."

Gemma's sarcastic laughter filled the closet. "Not from where I sit."

"I can explain it all. Please, allow me until the end of the week," Ralston pleaded.

Gemma swallowed through a tight throat. "I am afraid that is not possible. Either you tell me now or never."

"I cannot."

"Then, Lord Ralston, we have nothing more to say to one another." Gemma tried pushing him to the side.

He grabbed at her. "Gemma …"

The door behind them wrenched open, and Gemma squinted through the darkness to see Worth and Duncan filling the doorway. Their thunderous gazes spoke of the trouble she was in. Duncan had warned her of Ralston, and she'd chosen to ignore him. Now she must convince him not to inform Uncle Theo of her transgressions.

She pushed past Ralston. There was nothing left to discuss. When she passed him, he struck his arm out, halting her. He pulled a letter from his pocket and handed it to her. "This letter explains it all. After you read it and I still hold your love, send me a message. If I do not hear from you, I will keep my distance. But know this, I will not give up on our love," Ralston whispered in Gemma's ear.

Gemma glanced up and saw the sincerity in Ralston's gaze. Their kiss, his touch, the grief she heard in his voice for betraying her—all of it spoke volumes to her heart. She owed him enough to hear his explanation. She nodded before walking away. When she walked between Worth and Duncan, she saw Abigail waiting a few steps away, nervously glancing up and down the hallway. Gemma sighed. Her rash actions affected more than just herself. She'd risked Abigail's reputation too, not to mention Jacqueline's.

Her act of falling head over heels in love with Ralston and her belief in happily ever after placed her family at risk. Still, she couldn't stop her romantic fantasies where Ralston was concerned. She needed to proceed with caution. Gemma slipped his note in her dress and hooked her arm through Abigail's.

"Return the ladies to the box. I shall be along shortly," Worth ordered Forrester.

Forrester narrowed his gaze, looking back and forth between them, before glaring at Ralston. Ralston glanced away, feigning indifference and boredom. He was anything but. He wanted to roar his outrage at them for interrupting his time with Gemma before he could convince her to wait for him. Forrester stalked away to join the two ladies, ushering them back into the crowded hallway.

Worth shoved Ralston against the door. "What in the hell were you thinking? You promised to keep your distance from Gemma until we completed our mission."

"I tried, but her tortured gaze tore me apart. I needed to see her."

Anger flashed in Worth's eyes. "You have placed Gemma at risk once again for someone to call out her indiscretions. Not to mention if Lady Langdale found you in Gemma's company. We are almost to the finish line. When we complete this task, it will set us solid. Do not blow this. I have too much riding on it."

Ralston threw Worth off him. "As do I."

Worth grunted. "You do not act like it."

"Trust me. After this evening, Lady Langdale will agree to the sale of the coin," Ralston smugly flaunted.

"For your sake, she better," Worth threatened before strolling away.

Ralston straightened his clothing and closed the door. He stood waiting until Worth disappeared into the crowds before he followed. One would imagine Ralston felt the pressure from all sides not to screw up. However, he only held faith in his ability to succeed. The kiss he shared with Gemma set his doubts to the side and gave him the confidence he needed. The cocky smile gracing his face spoke it all.

When he stood outside his box and watched how comfortably Lady Langdale sat in his wealth, his grin turned devious. He wouldn't need a week. Lady Langdale would fall sooner than he had planned.

~~~~~~

"How silly of me. I am sorry for the misstep. I followed those ladies, assuming they were on their way to the retiring room. Thank you for saving me from my mishap." Gemma thanked Abigail.

"I warned you to stay away from that man," Duncan muttered for Gemma's ears alone.

"And I refused to listen," Gemma said calmly, her face spread in a friendly smile to those they passed.

Duncan's grip tightened on Gemma's arm as he guided them toward the nearest resting room. "Hurry about your business. I need to return you to our box before Uncle Theo sends out a search party."

"Why, of course, dear cousin," Gemma cooed before sweeping into the receiving room.

"Watch her," Duncan ordered Abigail.

"He is so fussy," said Gemma. "My absence was not long."

"He has reason to be, and yes, your absence was lengthy," Abigail stated, searching the room to confirm they were alone. Once she realized no one else was present, she rounded on Gemma to reprimand her. However,

Gemma had already lost herself in Ralston's letter. "Whatever were you thinking by sequestering yourself alone with Lord Ralston, where anyone could come upon you? Your actions could cause a scandal for *your* family."

Gemma ignored the question as her eyes devoured Ralston's penmanship. She hadn't taken in the words yet, only stared at the bold script flowing over the missive. The passion in his words leapt from the page without her even reading them. Her eyes focused on his signature. She traced over the letters, feeling the impact of Ralston by the letters alone.

"*Our* family," Gemma murmured absently.

My dearest Gemma,

Please forgive my absence over the past few days. The time has been agonizing without you. Do not trust the rumors of my status as a rake. I have not used you for my pleasure. I have only used you for my heart to beat as one with yours. Our night together was magical. There has been no other before who has awakened me to the pleasure as you have. And there will be no other from that night forth. You are my gem that I will treasure forever.

I must finish some business before I can ask Colebourne for your hand. I cannot go into much detail because of the circumstances involved. Most of my unpleasant business involves Lady Langdale. There is an item I must procure from the widow with undue haste. Once I have secured such item, we can begin our lives together.

You may over the next few days find me in acts with the widow that will cause you alarm. Please understand they are only actions I must perform and there is no truth behind them. I do not wish to cause you any heartache. Only happiness.

For my plan to find success, I must refrain from all contact. Also, if you could pretend your disinterest in my character, it would help my mission along. I will know your statements to be false because my heart holds yours as your heart holds mine. One day we shall have no need for secrecy. Our families will learn of our love for one another. I know we have not spoken the words. However, I do not need them spoken, for I know the strength of our connection. When we made love, our emotions formed an unbreakable bond of everlasting love.

Your dearest,
Barrett

Gemma finished the letter, a calming acceptance settling over her from what she'd witnessed earlier. She'd known in her heart that Barrett could explain his behavior. She didn't need to understand the full details of his involvement with Lady Langdale. Gemma held faith in Barrett and their love. Naïve or not, she trusted him.

"*Our* family, Abigail. When will you stop this nonsense of not believing that you are part of our family? It hurts my feelings that you hold yourself below us. You are my sister and I grow weary of your denials. If you continue with these denials, then I see no need to defend my actions to you any longer." Gemma's voice wavered at the end of her declaration. She didn't mean any of it. She only wanted Abigail to stop refusing her family's love. The letter crinkled in her fist in frustration.

Abigail gave her a sharp look. "Do not fool me with your threats. I am aware of how you are trying to change the subject to distract me from warning you against your actions. Actions that shall be your demise."

Gemma stood firm. "I meant what I said."

"Fine. Have it your way. But let it be known that I warned you." Abigail flew out of the room, distressed.

Tears formed in Gemma's eyes. She hadn't meant to hurt Abigail. She wanted her sister by her side. She wanted to share her happiness with the person she loved the most. However, Abigail had erected these walls around herself ever since Uncle Theo had announced his plans for the season. On every occasion, Abigail distanced herself more and more from the family. Gemma feared her comments this evening had pushed Abigail further away.

Gemma shoved the letter in her pocket, hurrying after Abigail to hopefully salvage what she could of their relationship. Not realizing the letter in its crumpled state hung from her pocket. When she brushed through the door, it fell to the floor.

Selina stepped out from behind the concealment hidden in the back of the room. Once Selina reached the door, she saw the letter lying on the floor. She lifted it and read the scandalous note. It detailed the love Lord Ralston held for Gemma. Selina gasped when she read that the two of them had made love. Then she read Ralston's plan for Lady Langdale and felt relief. Ralston meant to expose Lady Langdale for something. If he did, then it would draw away from her blackmail. Still, she needed to seek Duncan's advice with no one learning of her intent. She placed the letter in her reticule, intending to return the missive to Gemma, and hurried out the door to follow her.

Selina arrived breathlessly outside of Colebourne's box. Luck rested on her side once again this evening. Duncan stood outside after ushering Abigail and Gemma inside. Selina grabbed his arm, hoping to snare his attention. "I need to speak with you."

Duncan shook her hold off. "Not now, Selina."

"It is important. I must tell you something."

"It will have to wait."

"I have information about Gemma that could ruin her," whispered Selina.

Duncan shook his head in disappointment. "Will your vindictive nature never end? I believed your character stronger than your behavior. But each time you prove my faith otherwise. I do not understand why I even bother."

As much as his words stung, Selina needed to tell him of her predicament. Selina followed Duncan inside the box. Her argument hung on the tip of her tongue, ready to rock the very foundation of her future, when she noticed the occupants had focused their attention on her. She took a step back and tried to disappear from the box. However, the Duke of Colebourne was upon her before Selina realized the duke's intent.

"Had I known you and your father were to attend this evening's play, I would have extended an invitation to join us," said the duke.

Selina attempted a smile. "Father decided to attend at the last minute. Our relatives arrived in town, and he wanted to entertain them with the theatre since they do not have the same privilege in their village."

"Would your father mind if we steal you for the rest of the play? I would love to bend your ear on the set and the costumes."

Selina hesitated only a second. "I do not think he would care and I would love to. If you will allow me to pass a message to the footman assigned to me."

Colebourne nodded. "Excellent, tell the young fellow we shall escort you to your father after the play is over."

Selina nodded and passed the information to the footman. Before she walked back to the duke, she tried to attract Duncan's attention again. However, he turned his shoulder in a rebuke toward her. She tried not to let his cold regard hurt, but the ache still settled in her heart. She watched him join the other young ladies and gentlemen.

When Charlotte Sinclair made a quip to him, nodding her head at Selina, he snarled at her. Charlotte laughed loud enough for the others to question her. Whatever she replied had them laughing. A few of them covertly glanced at her, then quickly away when they noticed her stare. None of them offered for her to join them. Even her own fiancé ignored her. No, as usual, Gray's attention was focused on Abigail.

When the duke called her name, she found her seat next to him and answered each of his questions. Soon Selina relaxed under the duke's charm. It wasn't long before he had her laughing. As menacing as the rest of his family was toward her, he regarded her with kindness. He was the only highlight in her future when she married Lucas Gray. The only disappointing factor was Colebourne's age. His latest health issues only showed he might not live much longer. Which saddened Selina because of the tumultuous relationship she shared with her father.

Selina's glance veered over to Duncan and his cousins.

"It will not always be like this, my dear," Colebourne reassured her.

"Will it not?"

"No. Trust me when I say only brighter days are in your future."

"I do not see how. They will always hate me." Selina's lips pinched together.

"Perhaps if you show them a reason not to, they will no longer hold their animosity."

"What if I cannot?"

"I believe you are capable of better things to come. 'Tis only you who can make it happen." Colebourne patted her hand.

"What if I have information that could ruin one of your wards, but if I do not inform you, it will ruin my standing in society instead?"

Colebourne gave her question serious thought. "Then you must decide if how the ton views you is worth your integrity. Will ruining one of my wards gain you anything worthwhile?"

Selina shook her head. "No. But what can ruin me will also harm your family."

Colebourne nodded thoughtfully. "Then you must decide if the risk outweighs your happiness in the end."

"A decision with a tremendous amount of pressure to do the honorable thing."

"In which I believe you already know in your heart what you wish to do."

Selina looked down at her hands as she twisted them in her lap. "I know what I must do, but the party I need to inform refuses to speak with me."

Colebourne smiled. "You must try harder. You are a clever girl. Perhaps step back from what others expect of you and venture into unknown territory to spark this person's interest."

Selina thought over the duke's suggestion. Could she act so boldly? It would be completely out of character for her to do so. However, it would catch the gentleman unguarded. She needed her target to listen to her with no distractions.

"And if I cannot?"

Colebourne shrugged. "Then perhaps the person is not worth the effort. You will not know unless you try."

Selina sighed. "Either way, I am afraid scandal will strike our families."

"Ahh, never fear, my dear. We come from ducal families that when united, we only display our greatest strengths."

Selina nodded. The duke's attention turned toward the play in progress. Selina's gaze traveled around the box, taking everyone in. Gemma had her attention focused across the theatre on Ralston's box. The rest of the occupants were watching the play. Everyone except for Duncan. His attention centered on her, his gaze narrowed. Selina lifted her chin and pressed her shoulders back, refusing to cower under his regard.

Let him wonder what she was discussing with the duke. He'd had his opportunity and refused. She shifted her gaze back to Lord Ralston's box and encountered Lady Langdale's attention. She tilted her head toward the duke, and the widow's smile widened. Selina had planted the first seed. Now she only needed to plant the rest, then sit back and watch the beauty display itself as the duke suggested.

Chapter Twelve

The next morning, the breakfast table sat in an eerie silence, except for the noise of the utensils scraping against the plates. Gemma glanced around and saw the unhappy expressions on her family's faces. She knew her own expressed her misery. She'd tossed and turned all night at the cruel words she'd spoken to Abigail. Gemma wished she could take them back, but she couldn't. Still, it didn't stop her from hoping for Abigail's forgiveness.

Abigail had avoided her glances all morning. Gemma stopped by Abigail's bedroom to walk to breakfast with her as they usually did, but Abigail had already gone down by herself. When Gemma walked into the breakfast room, Abigail had seated herself between Jacqueline and Aunt Susanna.

"Was last night's entertainments too strenuous for you young people?" inquired Aunt Susanna.

"Perhaps we should curb their excitement and accept fewer invitations," Colebourne suggested.

Soon the table erupted into mindless chitter-chatter with their opinions on the play and the gowns the women wore to the theatre. Duncan and Lucas struck up a conversation about a horserace they wanted to attend. The duke smiled slyly at the reaction he hoped to receive from his comment. His son, nephew, and nieces were predictable. Now he only needed to plant his own seeds for them to flourish.

"It was gracious of Lady Selina to join us for the second half of the play. However, I am most disappointed by the welcome she received from my family. A welcome that must change. She will soon become a member of this family and deserves the same affection you regard one another with. Which is why I have arranged for a dinner party this Friday in Lady Selina's honor."

The room grew quiet again at his reprimand. He looked around the table and noticed the displeasure on his nieces' faces. Then he glanced at Lucas and saw how he longingly stared at Abigail. When he came upon Duncan, he watched the transformation on his face. His frustration built, and his hands curled into fists on the table. Colebourne wanted to chuckle but needed to keep his disappointment firm. He wondered how much longer Duncan would hold on to his resistance. Colebourne had invited Duncan to join them for the season for this very reason. He wanted the boy to suffer enough to chase the girl. However, after he witnessed Duncan's treatment of Lady Selina at the play, the boy needed to suffer a while longer.

"She was quite entertaining, and I enjoyed her companionship."

"Yes, Uncle, your conversation with the miss seemed quite intense. Did you learn anything interesting from Lady Selina?" asked Duncan.

Colebourne nodded. "Why, yes, I did, my boy. She offered me an interesting tad bit of information regarding my ward."

"Which ward?" squeaked Gemma.

"What information?" asked Duncan at the same time.

"Well, that is between Lady Selina and me."

Duncan slid his fork back and forth. "I am curious about what she shared with you."

Colebourne narrowed his gaze. "Then you should have granted her the time when she requested it. However, you only offered your indifference and a few scathing words. Words she did not deserve."

"She only wanted to tarnish Gemma's reputation," Duncan defended.

"How so?" asked Colebourne.

"It does not matter now. I am sure she fed you enough false information to punish Gemma."

"Is that so?" Colebourne shifted his attention toward Gemma. "Gemma, have you acted inappropriately where there is a need for tighter restrictions on your activities?"

Gemma gulped. "No."

"No?"

Gemma shook her head. "No, Uncle Theo. I promise I have done nothing to cause scandal on our family."

Gemma squirmed under her uncle's foreboding stare. She hated lying to him, but couldn't admit to every scandalous activity she had partaken in since she arrived in London. She feared they were more scandalous than Charlie's and Evelyn's ever were. How had Selina learned of her trysts with Ralston? And what had she whispered in her uncle's ear last night? Her curiosity grew the longer her uncle stayed silent.

"That is good to hear." Colebourne resumed eating, leaving his family wondering what he discussed with Lady Selina. Before he lifted his newspaper, *The Morning Post*, Duncan interrupted him.

Duncan cleared his throat. "You never mentioned what Selina spoke of Gemma."

Colebourne folded the paper closed. "No, I never did because Selina never even spoke Gemma's name."

"But …"

"But what, my boy?"

Duncan shifted under his uncle's bold stare. "You said she offered you information on your ward."

"Yes. However, I did not indicate which ward. You assumed it was about Gemma. Which leads me to believe a secret concerning Gemma is being kept from me. Since no one at this table wishes to share the secret, then I see no need to share the secret I learned from Lady Selina."

Goodwin spoke from the doorway. "Lady Noel and her brother Mr. Worthington are waiting in the foyer for Lady Gemma."

Colebourne stood. "Please inform them that Lady Gemma shall attend them shortly. If the rest of you will excuse me, I have a busy day ahead."

Uncle Theo left before anyone could get any more information from him. Gemma had felt stressed before breakfast, but now she was downright fearful. If her uncle didn't know of her secrets, he would soon. She hoped Ralston finished with his business before the ton learned of their secret rendezvouses.

"Gemma, do you have plans with the Worthingtons?" asked Aunt Susanna.

"Yes. I am sorry I forgot to mention Mr. Worthington wanted to take a carriage ride before his afternoon appointments and Noel agreed to accompany us. Is that all right?" Gemma twisted the napkin in her lap.

Aunt Susanna nodded. "Yes, dear. I am pleased your courtship with Mr. Worthington is moving along smoothly. Your uncle will find delight in this news too. There is no need for a maid or a footman to accompany you. Lady Noel should be a proper enough chaperone."

Gemma nodded and excused herself. She hoped if her uncle crossed paths with the Worthingtons, they would use a similar excuse. Gemma held no clue why they were paying her a visit this morning. Worth still clung to his fury with Ralston for sneaking her away. She'd suffered the rest of the play, listening to how foolish their actions were. It'd taken all her willpower to remain at the theatre and not plead a headache to return home. Between Abigail, Worth, and watching Ralston charm Lady Langdale, Gemma had endured all she could. How she kept her calm was beyond her.

"You look lovely today, Lady Gemma," complimented Worth.

Gemma nodded. "Thank you, kind sir."

"Are you ready for our ride?" asked Noel, bouncing on her feet.

"I only need to grab my bonnet and pelisse. If you will excuse me, I shall not be long."

Worth nodded, and Noel offered to accompany Gemma to her bedroom. Neither one of them spoke until they reached the comfort of privacy.

"I had hoped that would be the reason for your arrival. It was the excuse I gave my family for your appearance. Why are you here?" Gemma whispered.

Noel's grin widened. "It is a surprise. Hurry, we must not delay."

"What kind of surprise?"

"I cannot say. I made a promise. Will this one do?" Noel asked, picking up a bonnet lying on the chaise.

Gemma nodded, confused by the secrecy and their need to rush. She tried to question Noel further, but her friend wouldn't budge. She ushered Gemma from her bedroom, hooking her arm through her elbow. "Trust me. You shall soon see for yourself."

Once they reached the foyer, Goodwin held the door open for them to leave. When a footman followed to assist the ladies into the carriage, Worth refused his help. He explained that his own footman waited and pointed to the carriage. Once Uncle Theo's servant took notice of the footman by the carriage, he nodded and returned to the house. Gemma's confusion continued to grow over the secrecy.

Noel entered the carriage first. Before Gemma entered, she paused and took in the seriousness of Worth. Her curiosity grew even more intrigued.

"Please take your seat, Lady Gemma. We must leave with undue haste," urged Worth.

Gemma paused. "Why the need for such haste?"

Worth nodded at the conveyance. "If you enter the carriage, you will learn. Now, before a member of your family wishes to join us. For there is no room for an extra occupant."

He guided Gemma into the carriage. When she stepped inside, her gaze landed on Noel's animated face. Out of the corner of her eye, she noticed another occupant. A man sat opposite Noel. A gentleman of means by the footwear and attire. His fragrance wafted over Gemma, and she swung her head toward the gentleman. Lord Ralston sat with a smirk on his smug appearance. Gemma narrowed her eyes. Even though his letter had eased her fears, she still stood firm from when she left him the evening before.

"Take a seat, Gemma," Worth hissed from the doorway.

With a *humph*, Gemma sat next to Noel. Ralston's smirk dropped, replaced with a frown. Worth sat next to Ralston and tapped the roof of the carriage. Soon the conveyance took off. Gemma held no clue to the destination.

Gemma lifted her chin and avoided his gaze. "You promised you would wait for me to send word. I have sent none."

Ralston's voice deepened on his next words. "I could not wait a second longer to see you."

Gemma swung her gaze to meet his. "So you risk my reputation once again? Not to mention taking advantage of my friendship with the Worthingtons."

"Oh, he is not taking advantage of our friendship," interrupted Noel. "I made a promise that I would aid you in whatever way possible for time alone with Ralston."

"That was before, dear friend, the fiend flaunted his promiscuous relationship with a widow for the entire ton to see," Gemma hissed.

Ralston stretched his hands across the carriage, then pulled them back. "I explained myself in the letter. Did you not read the letter in its entirety?"

Gemma scoffed. "I read the letter. However, you explained no more in your letter than you did in the closet."

"Closet?" asked Noel with curiosity in her voice.

"Noel," Worth warned.

"You were alone in a closet. Where?" Worth's warning went unnoticed. Noel wanted details, but no one offered her any.

Gemma kept glaring at Ralston. As she lay in bed last night, she'd decided she wouldn't forgive Ralston until he was completely honest with her.

"Noel! I only brought you along for a cover. You promised not to ask questions," said Worth.

Noel sighed and sat back in the seat. She crossed her arms in front of her chest and pretended to pout. However, her curiosity got the better of her, and she kept glancing back and forth between Gemma and Ralston. Gemma knew that the first opportunity Noel got her alone, she would pepper her with questions until Gemma pacified her.

"He cannot explain more," offered Worth.

Gemma narrowed her gaze. "Why not?"

Worth pinned her with his stare. "Because the matter is sensitive. One that involves several key factors. Factors that, if they became exposed, can have a fallout of insurmountable damage. It is in your best interest not to know the full details. Basically, it comes down to how much trust you hold in Ralston. If you hold none, then the feelings you profess to have for him are a falsity to all those involved."

"That is enough," snarled Ralston. "You speak too harshly and out of line."

Worth shrugged. "Perhaps. However, I have come to care for Gemma as a friend. And as her friend, I only wish to protect her."

"That is not your position. 'Tis mine," growled Ralston

"And yet again, you are doing a poor job of it."

Ralston shot him a dirty look. "Get lost."

Worth laughed. "Hard to do since it is my carriage we ride in. Also, it is my job to keep you in line."

"How much longer before we reach our destination?"

Worth pulled out his timepiece and noted the time. "We should arrive there soon."

"And where exactly might *there* be?" Gemma arched a brow.

However, her question would go unanswered by everyone in the carriage. All the occupants refused to make eye contact with her. They looked out the windows, finding interest in the scenery of the crowded London streets. However, when Gemma took a glance, she noticed they were no longer in London, but had ridden into the open countryside. She glanced back at them to voice her objections, but their glances skidded away again.

It would appear everyone knew of their destination, except for her. And they would keep their silence until they reached it. While Gemma had left with them of her own free will, it would also appear they were kidnapping her too. Gemma relaxed in the seat once she realized her questions would go unanswered.

Soon, the carriage came to a halt. Gemma peered out the window again and noticed a tiny cottage nestled in between a gathering of trees and bushes. The carriage door opened, and the gentlemen exited. Gemma turned to Noel, who smiled with excitement over the clandestine journey. Noel patted Gemma's hand before disembarking. Which only left Gemma to do the same. Before she lowered her foot to the step, Ralston wrapped his hands around her waist and lifted her down. When her feet reached the ground, Ralston kept his arm wrapped around her waist and drew Gemma close.

Worth pulled out his watch again. "One hour and we depart."

Ralston nodded in agreement and drew her with him to the cottage. Gemma glanced over her shoulder to note Worth offering his arm to Noel. They strolled toward a path, leading them into a group of trees. Worth's servants walked around and stood on the side of the carriage facing the road, on guard. Gemma wondered about their seriousness. Were they in danger? Or were the gentlemen paranoid of her uncle following them? Which was preposterous.... Wasn't it?

When they entered the cottage, Gemma noted the quaint cottage's decor. Obviously, it was a rendezvous location for the gentlemen's philandering ways. A sense of disgust toward Ralston at bringing her to such a place overcame her. Each time she was alone with him, she discovered how little she understood his character. She pulled her arm from him and stopped in her tracks. She held no desire to indulge in the same pastimes he shared with other ladies.

Ralston felt Gemma's withdrawal since she entered the carriage. He had hoped his letter would have secured her trust, but apparently, he was mistaken. Now she stood offended for a reason Ralston was clueless to. He hurried into the room and straightened the mess around the sofa. He wanted to start a fire to warm the chill, but he couldn't afford to draw more notice to the cottage.

"Will you please take a seat?" he asked.

"No. I would like to leave."

"Will you not hear me out?"

Gemma gritted her teeth. "Anywhere but here."

Ralston looked around the cottage, confused at Gemma's disgust. Had he misjudged her? He knew the duke had pampered Gemma her entire life. However, he thought she was above the snobbery she displayed now. Perhaps he didn't know Gemma as well as he thought he did.

Ralston cocked his head to the side. "Do you feel you are above such lowly accommodations?"

Gemma wrinkled her nose. "No. The cottage is lovely. However, it is the state of its usage that clouds its charm."

Ralston chuckled once he realized why Gemma wanted to leave. He propped his elbow on the fireplace mantle, striking a comfortable pose. "And what usage do you imagine occurs here?"

Gemma *humphed*. "One that I shall not take part with you in."

Ralston clutched his heart. "Oh, the pain you strike me with."

Gemma turned to stalk away, but before she could, Ralston rushed forward and drew her into his arms. She stiffened against him. As much as he enjoyed teasing her, he needed to convince her to wait for him. Worth hadn't allowed him much time, so he couldn't waste any more. He lowered his head to take a nip at her neck. Gemma's body relaxed, and he thought he heard her sigh.

He placed a kiss on her neck before his tongue trailed a path of fire to her ear. "No woman has graced her presence here before. 'Tis only a place for Worth and me to meet without interruptions."

After he reassured Gemma, she melted in his arms. He pressed himself against her backside and pulled her tighter into his embrace. His lips traced down to the buttons on the back of her dress. His fingers made quick work of the top buttons, as his lips kissed her exposed skin. While he should explain his actions from the evening before, he couldn't stop himself from devouring Gemma. She was a drug his body had become addicted to. He promised himself after each button that it was the last one he would undo. However, his fingers kept moving, opening them one after another. When he reached her waist, Ralston slid Gemma's sleeves off her arms and turned her around.

Her creamy skin glowed from the sunlight that streamed in through the window. His fingers trailed up her arms, sliding the ribbons of her chemise off her shoulders. His mouth followed the path of his fingers across her shoulders, suckling on the spot where her neck curved for better access. Ralston's tongue dipped in between the valley of her breasts the corset kept pressed tightly together. While his mouth set Gemma's body aflame, he worked on the bindings of her corset, and soon he had the contraption unbound. Her breasts beckoned him to feast upon them.

Gemma had gone mad. Slowly. Irrevocably. Mad. She melted like a silly debutante at the whisper of Ralston's kisses. Were the other ladies he seduced as powerless? If so, she understood why they risked their reputations for him. She knew they must talk, but her body only sang with the need to have him fulfill her.

Gemma wanted Ralston to make love to her.

When the cool air hit her chest, she should have demanded that Ralston put a stop to his affections. Instead, she drew his head to her breasts. Her body ached for him to pleasure her. When his lips drew a nipple into his mouth, Gemma's knees buckled. Ralston lifted her into his arms and carried her to the sofa, never taking his mouth from her. He suckled her breasts, drawing her ache higher.

She moaned. "Ralston."

"Barrett," he growled.

"Barrett." She sighed. "Please."

"Please what?"

"Love me," she demanded.

When they reached the sofa, Barrett lifted his head and ravished Gemma's mouth, demanding the passion she so willingly gave him. She clutched at his hair, tugging him closer. She couldn't get enough of him. As much as he demanded, Gemma demanded more and lost herself in the decadence of pleasure.

Barrett tore at the buttons on the placket of his trousers, lowered them, and sat on the sofa, drawing Gemma onto his lap. He didn't give her time to question his motives—his hands drove between her thighs. Oh, sweet merciful heavens!

Gemma's body opened to him, drawing him deeper into her wetness. His fingers stroked and plied her body until a scream burst from her. Before she came down from her bliss, he coaxed her over his cock and slowly slid inside. She rocked him to his core. He closed his eyes and pressed himself up hard inside her. Gemma's hot wet pussy clutched at his cock, demanding that he fulfill her needs.

Her wanton display of indecency should have shocked Gemma, but the sensations swirling inside her demanded freedom. Freedom to give herself to Barrett with nothing but the love in her heart.

His hands tightened on her hips, and she wondered what she had to do to achieve his utter surrender. When he pressed upward again and swirled his hips under her, Gemma realized what she must do.

She rested her hands on his shoulders, her fingers digging into his shirtfront. She rose up, pressed her chest into Barrett's face, and then slowly slid back down. At his groan of pleasure, Gemma repeated the performance over and over again. Barrett released her hips and drew her breasts in his hands, pinching her nipples, increasing the ache between her thighs. When his mouth replaced his hands, Gemma lost all sense of sanity. Her pace increased with each tug of his lips around her nipples. Her body rocked against his, drawing them deeper into the abyss of satisfaction.

Barrett lifted his head from Gemma's bountiful breasts, her nipples teasing him to return to the sweet taste of cherries. However, his control kept slipping further and further away as Gemma rode his cock. He grabbed her neck, bringing her down for a kiss. Their gazes collided, and the love in her eyes shook what remained of his sanity. Her eyes were glazed over from the passion their bodies shared and her lips were plump from his kisses. Somewhere in their frenzy, Gemma had lost her bonnet, and now her hair tumbled around her shoulders.

Their bodies stilled with time, clinging in mid-air. Gemma trembled in his arms. They each waited, lost in the unknown.

Gemma drew an unwavering breath. Barrett's gaze reached down into her soul and drew her into his. She closed her eyes briefly, savoring the bliss of him deep inside her. When she opened them again, she pressed herself down onto him. Barrett lost control and surrendered everything that made him who he was and welcomed her into him.

Barrett drew in a shaky breath and gathered Gemma closer. She snuggled and pressed soft kisses to his neck, their hearts beating as one. He allowed himself to savor the memory before he lifted her chin and stole a kiss from her. She sighed and tried to pull him in deeper, but Ralston reluctantly pulled away.

"We must put your dress to rights before Worth and Lady Noel return from their walk."

"Must we?" Gemma teased.

Ralston moaned in frustration. "You, my dear, are a minx that tempts the very devil."

Gemma gave him a flirtatious look. "So you keep saying. Are you the devil, Lord Ralston?"

"I am only a saint walking amongst the wickedness of life."

Gemma laughed. "You, my lord, are the wickedness of them all. A rake of the highest order."

"Only with you, my love."

Ralston stood up with Gemma in his arms. He kissed her lips swiftly before sliding her down his body. After turning her around, he made quick work of putting her dress to rights. Then he sat back down with her on his lap. He wanted to hold her while he discussed why he'd brought her to the cottage.

"I have not slept with Lady Langdale, nor will I ever."

Gemma stiffened a little. "Then why the display of affection?"

Ralston sighed. "It is beneficial for a mission I must complete."

Gemma brushed her fingers across his cheek. "Are you a spy?"

Ralston laughed. "No. If so, my assignment would be much simpler."

"I do not understand. Who do you work for? And why? You are a marquess, heir to a duke."

Ralston nodded. "Yes. However, that role does not offer me the same fulfillment as the partnership I am involved with."

"With Worth?"

"Yes."

Gemma blew out a breath. "And I suppose you can tell me no more?"

"At this time, no."

"And when can you?"

Ralston shrugged. He had no definite date on when he could confide in Gemma. If ever. Ralston was still trying to convince Worth they could trust her with their secret. Worth stood firm on his answer. The only way he would relent would be if Gemma were Ralston's wife. A feat that Ralston kept getting denied at every turn.

"Very well." Gemma placed a soft kiss on Ralston's lips.

Ralston deepened the kiss before reluctantly pulling away. "Very well?"

"Very well."

Ralston frowned. "May I ask …?"

"I shall place my trust in your hands and wait patiently until the day when you can speak freely with your intentions. For the time being, I shall show my distaste for your presence if that will aid in your deception."

Ralston pressed his forehead against Gemma's. "You are amazing."

Gemma smirked. "I know."

Ralston laughed and relaxed back against the cushions, enjoying the opportunity to hold Gemma in his arms for a few peaceful minutes. They interlocked their fingers and cherished the simplicity of the quietness. Before long, Worth and Noel could be heard laughing outside the window.

Ralston and Gemma made their way outside, holding hands. Ralston entered the carriage first, in case anyone was traveling on the road and saw him. When Gemma entered, Ralston pulled her down on the seat next to him. Once they took off again, Gemma glanced at her friends, and Noel beamed at the love glowing from Gemma. However, Worth's frown spoke volumes about the turbulence of their relationship.

Gemma noted Worth was fighting with his honor at allowing himself to be caught in the middle of Ralston and Gemma's affair. As much as Gemma tried to reassure Worth, he remained unconvinced that Ralston was in her best interest. Even Noel tried to convince him, but he brushed his sister's arguments away, claiming her romantic nature didn't understand the realities of life.

The entire time, Ralston kept his hold on Gemma's hand, displaying his true intention, never once offering an argument against Worth. It was then that Gemma realized Ralston didn't feel the need to justify the depth of their relationship to a soul.

Therefore, neither did she.

Chapter Thirteen

Gemma walked alongside Abigail after breakfast. Gemma wanted to apologize for her harsh words at the theatre, but Abigail had avoided her at every opportunity. Gemma missed her friend and confidant.

That night had cast an uncomfortable silence in their household. Uncle Theo's reprimand rang clear. Gemma didn't understand why the rest of the house remained melancholy. Each occupant appeared deep in thought and was miserable for company.

Abigail walked ahead of Gemma toward a bench near the pond. Gemma followed and sat next to her, gazing at the ducks waddling by. Both girls turned toward each other and spoke at the same time.

"I am sorry—" said Gemma.

"Please forgive me—" said Abigail.

Both girls started laughing and hugged each other. They each started talking again. Gemma nodded her head to let Abigail speak first.

Abigail took a deep breath and plunged on. "Ever since your uncle announced his plans for the season, I have been a bore. The offer made me reflect on my standing in life and with your family. I admit I was perfectly content with the life he offered me over the years, and like a fool, I believed it would last forever. However, I have awakened to the reality of life and realized it is only a fantasy I created. I must face my future. One in which to keep my sanity shall be very far away. For I cannot watch Lucas marry

Selina. Already my heart aches for something that was never mine to begin with."

Gemma's heart hurt for her friend. "Oh, Abigail."

Abigail frowned sternly. "I do not want your pity, Gemma Holbrooke."

Gemma shook her head. "It is not pity I offer, Abigail Cason. I offer my love and support. Since falling in love with Ralston, I understand how agonizing it must be for you to watch the man you love commit to another and the heartache you must endure."

"It gets harder every day." Abigail sighed.

Gemma reached for Abigail's hand. "I am sorry you suffer. However, you are not alone. I want you to understand and accept that we are your family and we wish only the very best for you."

Abigail nodded. "Then once the season ends, will you help me convince the duke to allow me to take a position up north?"

"How far up north?" Gemma winced.

"Scotland."

"On the border?"

Abigail shook her head. "No. The Highlands."

Gemma made a sound of protest. "Abigail, no."

Abigail met her gaze, and Gemma saw determination. "Yes. I must go as far away as I can until the heartache eases."

"Will you return?"

"Yes."

Gemma stared at Abigail, trying to determine if she spoke the truth. Would Abigail return? Or was this her attempt to start anew? A fresh start where no one knew her status and accepted Abigail for herself, not for her lineage. Gemma didn't think Abigail realized the impact she had made on their family. She held the opinion that she was a servant, but in truth, Gemma's family loved Abigail dearly and considered her one of them. Gemma blamed Lucas for instigating doubts in Abigail's head and heart. His behavior toward her as of late had been atrocious.

"I promise to help you, if in return you make me a promise." Abigail nodded, and Gemma narrowed her gaze. "I want you to promise you will give the rest of the season a chance. You will attend every event and attempt to enjoy yourself."

"I promise."

She knew Abigail only promised so Gemma would support her. Which only upset her more. Abigail should already know Gemma would move heaven and earth for her. Abigail didn't need to make promises. She only needed to ask.

"All right. I will help convince *our* uncle of your decision."

Abigail smiled at Gemma's reference to Uncle Theo. Then she surprised her by jumping up and pulling at Gemma to rise. "If I am to embrace the London season, then I must try a flavored ice. Only, of course, to understand the craze for them."

Gemma laughed. "Of course."

Their laughter followed them on the walking trail. It drew many gentlemen's gazes their way. Many tipped their hat to them or bowed. Which only caused them to giggle more. Their joy caused many to smile, except for two ladies who watched from afar. They each stared with jealously, but one also held a wistful longing that would never be granted.

~~~~~

"Neither of them shall find much to laugh over soon."

Selina stayed quiet, not wanting to draw attention to herself with Lady Langdale. They sat in a closed carriage, but the curtains were open for any passerby to look inside. She didn't hold the same opinion as the widow. In fact, after their meeting was over, Selina meant to warn the duke of the widow's plan. Selina accepted her fate was one she held no favor for. However, she wouldn't allow another lady to succumb to the same fate. Being forced into a marriage where one held no affection for their spouse spelled a lifetime of loneliness.

"What is your plan?" asked Selina.

"Do you not mean to ask what I require from you?"

Selina shrugged.

Lady Langdale laughed. "I am glad to see that you have accepted your role in the demise of the Holbrooke chit."

"You have given me no other choice if I am to keep my name from any whisper of scandal."

"We shall make grand confidants in the years to come. I see myself in you. Your need for rank, prestige, and power run through your veins as they do mine." Under Selina's grimace, Lady Langdale nodded. "I made the horrid mistake of marrying my first husband, believing any link to the peerage would be enough to drag myself out of the utter despair I lived in. If I had known the order of the peerage, I would have pursued a higher rank."

Selina snarled. "Well, that is where we differ. I was born into my rank, and once I marry, I shall only secure it more so."

"Only if my lips stay sealed."

Selina kept her shudders locked inside. While she had been vindictive in the past, she held distaste for the lady sitting across from her. Hearing the comparison only made Selina's decision to confess more dire. After spending time in Lady Langdale's company, Selina wanted to atone for her past grievances with Colebourne's family. She wanted them to welcome her with their acceptance. To laugh with them. To feel sorrow with them. To belong in their embrace.

"What is it you require me to do?" asked Selina.

"After you drop my latest tidbit into the duke's ear and I read Mr. Worthington and Lady Gemma's wedding banns, I shall relinquish my threat against your person."

Selina narrowed her gaze. "You will no longer hold this threat over my head?"

"The threat will only hold if the two do not wed."

"And the information you wish for me to divulge?"

Lady Langdale leaned forward, whispering, "That you heard the most awful rumor of Lady Gemma reentering Mr. Worthington's carriage near a cottage outside of London earlier this week."

"Does this rumor hold any truth?"

"Yes." Lady Langdale's smile turned more devious.

With this piece of information, Selina grew confused about Gemma's relationship with Mr. Worthington. Had there been other occupants in the carriage? Or had they been alone? If so, was Gemma fickle about love and was trifling with two gentlemen this season? Selina had heard Gemma was a romantic. Did her naivety misunderstand the attention the gentlemen paid her? Two gentlemen whose rakish ways were well-known. She wasn't Gemma's friend, but she wished to warn her.

Selina pinched her lips. "All right. Tomorrow evening, my father and I are attending a dinner at their home. I will inform Colebourne of his niece's secret love tryst."

"Excellent."

"Now, please tell your driver to return me to my carriage."

Lady Langdale smirked at Selina's order. Once they reached her carriage, Selina wanted to hurry into hers. But before she closed the door, Lady Langdale laid down one last threat. "Do not think to double-cross me. I make a most unfortunate enemy."

Selina paled. "I would never dare to think otherwise."

Selina climbed into her carriage with her footman's help. Once she sank into the seat, her body trembled from the shudders she could no longer keep contained. Selina's future hung in the unknown.

After a while, her fear disappeared. Selina felt a lightness she hadn't ever experienced before. A sense of thrill coursed through her veins. No longer the heavy weight of the future clung to her shoulders, but the awakening of a chance for a carefree future filled with love.

~~~~~~

Ralston stood in the shadows of the alleyway and watched Lady Selina disembark from Lady Langdale's carriage. When the man he had assigned to tail Lady Langdale's every move sent a messenger to come to this location, he'd expected a menial report of the widow shopping and her countless visits to the other ladies in society who never climbed much higher than herself.

Instead, he now waited with bated breath as he watched the interaction between a lady as highborn as Lady Selina and the widow. Two unlikely cohorts he'd ever seen.

When Lady Selina exited the carriage, Lady Langdale threatened her. Lady Langdale held something over the young miss. And Ralston knew exactly what it was. And it didn't bold well for his future with Gemma.

He ordered the man to keep his eyes on the widow and thanked him for the latest development. Ralston needed to find Worth. They needed to alter their plan for Lady Langdale. His time to lure the widow into his trap had run out. He had made a mess of this assignment because of his obsession with Gemma. Before he ruined any more lives, he needed to fix his mistakes. If the ton learned of the blackmail Lady Langdale held over Lady Selina, the consequences would cause scandal for the prestigious families involved. Not only would it ruin the lives of the parties involved, but it would also ruin the innocent members of their families, leaving future generations to withstand the aftermath.

Too much stood at stake.

Ralston cut down the alleyways to his destination. With their money pooled together, he and Worth had purchased the plain house in Covent Garden. It fit in perfectly with their plans. Its plainness blended in with the other homes. He stormed inside and found Worth with his feet up on a desk, smoking a cigar.

Ralston swept Worth's feet down and snagged the cigar, stubbing it out in the ashtray. He stormed to the window and opened it to air out the cloudy room. "We agreed. No cigars unless the client lights one," Ralston reprimanded.

Worth smirked. "Hello to you too."

"A problem has developed."

Worth raised his feet back to the desk, indifferent to Ralston's snarl. His partner had kept pushing the boundaries with him ever since he refused to back away from Gemma. Worth sought his revenge by performing every irritating act he could think of. Ralston wanted to scream in frustration, but he had to pick his battles with Worth.

Ralston strode to the cabinet and pulled out two tumblers and a bottle of whiskey. He poured them each a shot. He threw his back quickly and poured another. Worth never lifted his. It was probably for the best if one of them remained sober.

"Every issue is a problem with you, Ralston."

Ralston whirled to face him. "Well, this one could determine the success or failure of our latest assignment. If we fail, then we cannot take our business to the legit level we wish to achieve. Instead, we shall be forever in the debt of men like Colebourne who will use us to their advantage."

Worth dropped his feet, adopting a more serious expression. "Explain."

"Samuel sent a message to meet him at his post. I thought he wanted to give me an update on Lady Langdale's agenda. Instead, I witnessed Lady Selina exiting Lady Langdale's carriage. The widow issued a threat to the duke's daughter."

Worth frowned. "What kind of threat?"

Ralston crossed his arms. "A threat to not cross her."

"What information does the widow hold over the debutante?"

Ralston winced. "That is where the problem lies."

Worth growled. "What have you done now?"

"It is not what I have done now, but more like what I did when I stole Gemma away at the Kanfold Ball."

"The one where Evelyn and I came to Gemma's rescue? The one where you abandoned her after risking her reputation?"

Ralston nodded. "The very one."

"Explain," Worth gritted out from between his teeth.

Ralston grimaced. "I might have forgotten to divulge that Lady Langdale followed us, with Lady Selina not too far behind. I lost the widow. However, Lady Selina might have encountered Forrester, who might have caught a glance of mine and Gemma's embrace. Forrester then caused a scandal with Lady Selina with his own passionate embrace. While sneaking out of the garden, I noticed Lady Langdale skulking in the shadows. I pretended not to see her. I imagined she got caught up in their tryst and forgot about following me. However, I have an eerie sense she is blackmailing Lady Selina and seeks to avenge her bruised heart at our expense."

Worth shook his head in disgust. "Lady Selina did not set out to have a tryst with Forrester, but Forrester forced her into one, so he could cover for Gemma. A fine mess you have made."

"What are we to do?" Sighing, Ralston ran a hand through his hair.

"We?" Worth scoffed. "No, my friend. I am finished cleaning up your messes. You will make a call on the lovely widow and seduce her this evening. After you bed her, she will give you the coin."

Ralston immediately disagreed. "No! I will not bed her."

"You have no choice." Worth pounded his fist on the desk.

"I will not betray Gemma for any plausible reason."

"The duke will destroy you if he does not receive that coin in two days. Any chance of claiming Gemma's hand, Colebourne will refuse. There is no other way."

Ralston stood firm. "Then he can destroy me. Gemma and I will be together."

"Like hell!" Worth exploded from his chair and advanced on Ralston. He shoved Ralston against the wall and grabbed him by the cravat.

Worth leaned into Ralston's face, and when he spoke, spit flew out of his mouth at each word. "You will not ruin what we have built over the last few years. Especially for some debutante you chased so you could play under her skirt. A fascination you will grow bored with as soon as the chase is over. I have seen it happen countless times. Your rank secures your position in society, while I have none. This is my chance to get out from under Reese's thumb. You will not deny me this opportunity. You will bed the widow."

Ralston threw Worth off him and swiped his face. "Why must I bed the widow to retrieve the coin? There must be another way. Or is this a chance for you to claim Gemma for yourself? I have seen you flirting with her at every opportunity you find. You are jealous that she has chosen me and cannot wait to flaunt my unfaithfulness in her face. Why? So you can pick up the pieces like a swell friend?"

Ralston strode over to the desk and poured himself another drink. However, one wasn't enough. He grabbed the bottle and drank from it as he paced back and forth. If he thought the whiskey would give him the answer to his dilemma or the courage to deal with his problems, he was sorely mistaken.

He understood Worth's need to break free from his family's control. Ralston himself suffered the same affliction, though not to the degree of Worth. His friend held no rank, only the standing of having an earl for a brother. On the other hand, Ralston was set to inherit a dukedom. There was no need for him to work.

However, the work he did with Worth helped him to keep a grip on his sanity. He wasn't one to idly sit by with no purpose to his days. No, he needed to keep busy. Plus, he enjoyed the work they did. When the day came for him to take on the role of a duke, he would step aside.

Ralston's mind scrambled to find a solution. He knew what he must do, but his heart wouldn't allow him to betray Gemma.

"You are wrong," said Worth, and Ralston paused and arched a brow. "I do not want Gemma."

"Humph."

Worth sighed and sat back in the chair. "I will not lie that she intrigued me when I first met her. She was fun to flirt with, but we never shared a spark of attraction. I regard her as a friend, nothing more. Then my best mate fell for her. You changed into an honorable gentleman."

Ralston looked confused. "You make it sound like an undesirable trait."

"On the contrary, Gemma brings out the best in you. I only hold happiness for your future with her."

"Then why force me to bed the widow?"

Worth shrugged. "It was a test to see how dedicated you are."

Ralston crossed his arms across his chest. "I refuse to follow your request."

"Then we need to brainstorm a solution for this mess. Put the bottle away."

Ralston nodded. "I do regret the mess I have made."

Worth sighed. "I know, but it is what one should expect from a bloke in love."

"I promise it will all end well," said Ralston.

"For your sake, I hope so."

Chapter Fourteen

Lady Langdale sat in the opulent room, waiting for the Duke of Colebourne to answer her call. If she thought they would grant her an audience with the duke in a parlor near the front of the house, she'd been mistaken. The servant walked her to a parlor where no other visitors would note her presence. If they thought to offend her, they failed. Instead, a sense of power consumed her at the threat they took her for.

The duke's wealth shone throughout his home in a tasteful manner. Soft yellows decorated the parlor she waited in. To make the atmosphere more welcoming, personal trinkets of the family were scattered about. Perhaps she had jumped to the wrong opinion of why they had sequestered her here.

However, it appeared they had forgotten about her. When the clock struck three, she realized she had waited for over two hours. Her fury unraveled, and she refused to wait another minute. If the duke chose to regard her so callously, then she would sell the coin he so eagerly sought. She rose in a huff at the exact moment the door opened. The scowl on her face quickly disappeared at the duke's appearance.

Colebourne rushed forward. "I am sorry for the delay."

Lady Langdale curtsied. "It is fine. I thank you for agreeing to see me."

Colebourne held out his arm, indicating for the widow to resume her seat. When Goodwin had informed him of her visit, he drew out visiting with her until she'd worked herself into a frenzy. Her visit surprised him and left him to wonder why someone as lowly as her thought he would welcome her into his home, especially considering the grave injustice her husband had committed toward his family.

For her to show herself here only meant one thing.

She hoped to humble herself before justice forced her to reveal her dead husband's role in the thievery of a valuable family coin, one that King Henry V had gifted Colebourne's ancestor.

Colebourne sat across from Lady Langdale, relaxing back to put the widow at ease. He smiled graciously at her and made polite conversation enough to charm her and make her relax in his company. When the clock announced the next hour, Colebourne could no longer delay. He was an important man who needed to instigate his plans before his family hosted a dinner the following evening.

"Now, what has brought about your visit?" asked Colebourne.

Lady Langdale sniffled, drawing a handkerchief to dab at her eyes. "I have begun to clear away my late husband's remains and found something of importance that I believe belongs to your family."

"Did your husband not pass over four years ago?"

"Yes. However, at his passing, I had been too distraught to clear them away."

Colebourne nodded. "That is understandable. It is very hard to lose a loved one."

"Yes. Even one with the reputation my husband held."

The duke refused to comment on the widow's description of the late baron, a man who had thieved at every house he'd received an invitation to.

Lady Langdale played the wronged widow to perfection, even when she was the guilty party who had led her husband to a life of crime.

Barbara Langdale was West End scum who had taught her husband how to fleece from his fellow peers.

Then once he died, she'd sunk her claws into Reese Worthington. Worthington had been, and probably still was, clueless about his mistress's actions. Once Worthington passed over the widow for Evelyn, Lady Langdale had become desperate to support herself. That was when Colebourne hired Ralston to entice the widow into an affair to regain the coin. However, Gemma had distracted Ralston from doing his job. It was now a mess he needed to fix, and he would do so tomorrow evening at dinner.

Lady Langdale pulled out the coin and handed it over to Colebourne. He brought the coin up to inspect the authenticity of it. It wasn't a replica. The marks and code on the coin proved it to be the original. He kept his expression stoic, not wanting the widow to see his relief at securing the coin back into the family's fold. She must have sensed her time had run out. It would only be a matter of days before her exposure to the ton led her to a cell in Newgate. "I cannot offer you a reward for an item stolen by your husband."

Lady Langdale shook her head. "Nor would I accept one, Your Grace. I only attempt to right a wrong."

Colebourne nodded and rose. He turned to leave, but Lady Langdale stopped him. "Your Grace, another moment, please."

Colebourne turned, sliding the coin into his pocket. He rested his hand on the back of the chair and pasted a smile of patience on his face, even though he grew weary of the widow's act.

"I am not one to gossip. However, I feel I owe you a debt of gratitude for not ruining my reputation with my husband's past actions. Therefore, I must inform you of a sight I caught yesterday afternoon on my ride through the countryside."

"And what might that sight be?"

Lady Langdale smiled sympathetically. "I witnessed your niece, Lady Gemma, entering a carriage with Mr. Worthington. They had just exited a cottage nestled in between some trees. Other carriages traveled the same path, and soon rumors will spread."

Colebourne stepped forward and offered Lady Langdale help in rising from her chair. He patted her hand and led her to the door. Before the door opened, he smiled at her. While the widow annoyed him with her innocent act, she'd just offered him the exact information he needed to implement his plan. Just when he thought his matchmaking attempts had resulted in a complete failure, a small crumb teased at his success.

"Not to worry, Lady Langdale. I hope you can keep a secret. Tomorrow evening, I am having a family dinner where I shall announce Gemma and Mr. Worthington's engagement. The couple wished to keep their love to themselves until the season ended. But I learned of their secret tryst and convinced them we must declare their love with much haste. Can I trust you to stay silent until I can have the banns read?" The duke whispered his request to emphasize the need for secrecy.

"Mum is the word."

A gleeful expression lit the widow's eyes, and Colebourne knew why. She thought Gemma was out of the picture and she could now sink her claws into Ralston. She was in for a grave disappointment once she declared her gossip to Ralston. Colebourne dropped her hand and ordered the footman to show Lady Langdale out.

He pulled the coin from his pocket and flipped it in the air. Oh, he loved when a grand plan came together. After tomorrow's dinner, Gemma's match would find success. Then he could lure his next victims into his mad matchmaking schemes.

Chapter Fifteen

Ralston knew what he risked by sneaking into Colebourne's residence, but the rewards would be worth it.

It had been two days since he'd seen Gemma and drunk from her succulent lips. Most men risked their freedom for the thrill of getting caught, making the tryst more exciting. Ralston risked his freedom in the name of love, an emotion he never thought he would feel for another. He'd scoffed at other men when they confessed their undying devotion to a woman. Now he understood why they always wore silly grins on their faces, making them look like fools. It was a group he was now a proud member of.

He tried to fool himself that he needed to warn Gemma about Lady Selina and Lady Langdale, but in truth, his trek through the shadows of the duke's garden was for his own selfish reasons.

Once he reached the house, he breathed a sigh of relief that no one had caught him. Ralston slipped through the secret entrance and made his way to Gemma's bedchamber. Luck remained on his side. Again, no one caught him.

He noticed a sliver of light under the secret opening and smiled. Gemma was still awake. Ralston pressed a button, and the door slowly opened. Gemma was at the vanity, brushing her golden locks. The brush coasted along the waves with gentle strokes. She hadn't noticed his arrival, and he gazed at her, taking in her beauty, searing the memory into his soul.

As she brushed her hair, Gemma lost herself in the memory of Barrett making love to her. Gemma's heart strained at the seams, wanting to burst from the emotions he stirred in her. She ached for him to hold her in his arms and reassure her that all would be well.

She feared Uncle Theo planned to make an announcement about her future tomorrow night at dinner. Between Aunt Susanna's inquiring questions concerning Gemma's feelings toward Worth and how they had invited the entire Worthington family to join them tomorrow evening, Gemma only fretted more. Uncle Theo had questioned Gemma about her carriage ride with Noel and Worth, leaving her wondering if he had learned of her secret meeting with Barrett.

A warm sensation overcame Gemma when she recalled the sensuous kiss Barrett had given her before she disembarked from the carriage. The heat in Barrett's gaze had reflected his love, leaving Gemma feeling secure.

She gasped when she lifted her head, and her gaze connected with the man consuming her thoughts. His intense stare stripped Gemma naked with his passionate need. Barrett stood at the entrance to the secret passageway and held out his hand. She rose and floated to his side, where he wrapped her in his embrace. Neither one of them spoke. The air stilled around them, waiting for the whisper of their kiss.

Barrett pulled back and brushed his knuckles down her cheek. He worked to control his baser needs. The need to take her pulled against his resistance. He closed his eyes and leaned his forehead against hers. Taking a deep breath, he relaxed, but when he opened his eyes to see the same depth of passion in Gemma's gaze, he almost lost himself in her. However, his willpower stood strong.

For now, at least.

"Do you trust me?"

Gemma nodded. Her emotions, too close to spilling over the edge, kept her silent.

Barrett pressed a soft kiss against her lips to let her know he felt the same. He grabbed her hand and led her along the passageway back outside, where he lifted her into his arms.

"Barrett," Gemma whispered.

"Shh, love."

Barrett ran through the garden with Gemma's dressing gown blowing behind them. Gemma giggled at the mischievous smile on Barrett's lips. When he entered the bedroom, his seriousness had stopped her heart. She'd feared what he might say to her. Her heart couldn't take it if he denied their love. Instead, he was showing Gemma a side of him she'd never seen before. A silly side full of mischief.

Oh, the consequence of getting caught with a rakehell of the ton carrying her through her uncle's garden in her nightwear screamed scandal like no other. But it would be one she would cherish for her remaining days. Because it was filled with love.

"Where are you taking me?"

"On an adventure."

Gemma laughed softly, loving the tone of Barrett's voice. He bundled them into an unmarked carriage, and they took off along the London streets. Barrett kept Gemma on his lap, settling them back in the seat. Gemma snuggled and wrapped her arms around him, her head nestled against his neck, and he rested his chin on top of her head. They rode in silence, listening to the sounds from the horses' hooves clomping along the streets and the noises from the night echoing around them. They needed no words, only the sound of their hearts beating as one.

Soon the carriage stopped, and Barrett drew Gemma outside. They'd arrived at another home as grand as her Uncle Theo's. While her uncle preferred to live in the city, this home sat on a magnificent estate outside of London. Their ride wasn't long to have traveled very far. The carriage had driven them to the rear of the estate.

Barrett gave the driver an order that Gemma didn't catch because she couldn't take her eyes off the splendid view. It didn't take her long to realize Barrett had brought her to his family's estate.

Which only increased the danger of their adventure.

Barrett lifted her in his arms again and walked along a path that led through a trail of trees to an open meadow with a pond. Lanterns hung from a tree with a picnic sitting nearby. Barrett carried Gemma to the blanket and slid her along his body. The air crackled around them. Before she could reach up to kiss him, he pulled them down and laid back with her in the crook of his arm.

Barrett lay with one arm under his head and the other wrapped around Gemma next to him. She wanted to kiss him, but Barrett wanted to give her an evening he'd cheated her from by not courting her properly. He'd let his passion for this mere slip of a girl consume him until his need had dominated the relationship. He wanted to give her this memory to cherish.

"Have you ever had a midnight picnic under the stars?"

Gemma smiled. "No."

"A first for both of us."

"You, the most sought-after rake of London, has never taken part in such an event? I find that difficult to believe." Gemma rolled on top of Barrett and propped her chin under her hands.

Barrett reached out to stroke a strand of Gemma's hair, rubbing it between his fingers before he slid it behind her ear. "Why?"

"Because you're you."

He chuckled lowly. "That is not a good enough answer."

"Because this setup is a classic seduction scene for a scoundrel."

Ralston gasped. "A rake and a scoundrel. Why, Lady Gemma, you hold a high opinion of my scandalous character."

Gemma paused before answering, afraid she'd offended Barrett. Their conversation had started out in a teasing nature, but he no longer smiled. Gemma had been about to apologize when she noticed his devilish eyes twinkling with laughter.

She swatted him on the shoulder. "For shame, my lord, for giving me doubt."

Barrett laughed, rolling them over, and stroked his fingers along Gemma's side, tickling her. Gemma let out a roar of laughter unbefitting of a lady and squirmed under his hold. Wanting to hear more, he trailed his finger along her side, keeping his ministrations up near her elbows. He laughed when her giggles turned into a snort that set her laughing harder.

However, when his fingers trailed to the curve behind her knees, she gasped and sighed at his caress. Since she was so ticklish everywhere else, he assumed she would be there too. Instead, she melted under his touch. The laughter in her eyes turned dark with desire. When she reached up to pull his head down for a kiss, he didn't deny her. He opened his mouth under hers willingly.

Gemma's kiss was soft, exploring Barrett with her innocence. Even though he'd taken her virtue with his seductive ways, she still held an innocence that endeared him to her. He hoped she would always hold this part of herself to pass on to their children.

She slid her hands through his hair and along his neck, her touch as light as a feather. He trembled above her.

Barrett's trembles set Gemma's heart racing. She knew he held himself back, but she didn't want him to. She wanted him to seduce her, but she knew his reasons for bringing her this evening meant more to him than seduction. His attempt to romance her endeared him to her. She hoped he kept surprising her with romance throughout their marriage. It was silly to think their lovemaking would lead to marriage, but Gemma's heart knew there was no other course for them to take.

She dragged her lips away, savoring the last of their kiss. "If this is not a seduction scene, then, pray tell, what is it?"

"A recreation of our last picnic together, where I behaved like a total arse. I wish to make it up to you."

"Oh, Barrett." Tears came to Gemma's eyes at his thoughtful gesture, and she fell for him harder. A tear leaked out, sliding along her cheek.

Barrett swiped at the tear with this thumb. "Your tears were not what I had in mind by redeeming myself."

"They are if they fall because of your sweetness."

"Then I shall allow them."

Barrett rolled off Gemma and pulled her into a sitting position. He tugged the picnic basket closer, opened the lid, and pulled out an assortment of foods. Each of the dishes was a replica of their picnic during the house party. He pulled the cover off a plate of shortbread with cherry glazing and popped one into Gemma's mouth.

Gemma moaned. "These taste like our chef's biscuits."

"Mmm." Barrett savored one for himself. "Perhaps because they are."

"How?" Gemma's eyes widened.

He smiled mischievously. "I might have charmed the recipe from your chef and perhaps a few other of your favorites."

"When?"

"During the house party when I came to a realization."

"And what was that?"

Barrett winked. "That I had fallen heads over heels for a chit out of my grasp and I needed whatever arsenal I could get my hands on to capture her."

"Mmm, that was not the impression you gave. In fact, if I recall, you found every reason to avoid me."

"A misunderstanding, 'tis all."

Gemma laughed over their silliness, and Barrett smiled widely over their mischief. He kept feeding Gemma and asked her questions he would have had he courted her properly. In return, he answered every question she asked, even the ones on a more personal level pertaining to his reputation. He held nothing back, offering her a full look at his character. He only hoped she found no fault with it to discourage their future. When she wrapped his hand in hers while they talked, Barrett relaxed.

They laid back down with Barrett holding Gemma and continued to talk with the moon shining high above and the stars twinkling down on them. They wished upon a star that shot from the sky.

"What did you wish for?" Barrett asked.

"I cannot tell or it will not come true," Gemma teased.

When he whispered in her ear of his wish, Gemma stood up. She dropped her robe, pulled her nightgown off, and stood before him naked in the moonlight. She held her hand out to him, and he rose with her.

Gemma took her time removing Barrett's clothing. With each button undone, she brushed her lips across his exposed skin. Once he pulled his shirt off, Gemma's fingers trailed patterns across his hardened abdomen, dipping in and out of his ridges. Barrett stood still, never moving a muscle while she explored. The only reaction betraying his unsteadiness was the deep breaths he took after her caresses stroked across his heated skin.

Gemma wanted Barrett to lose control and ravish her the way she desired. He may have whispered his wish, but he didn't believe she would make it come true. She planned to and more. With a seductive smile, she lowered to the ground, unbuttoned the placket of his trousers, and drew them down. Her mouth followed the trail of them hitting the ground. Soft kisses traveled back up until they reached his hardness.

"Gemma," Barrett growled, trying to pull her up.

However, before he could tighten his grip, Gemma slid her tongue along the length of him, and his knees almost buckled out from underneath him. When her warm mouth drew him inside, he closed his eyes, moaning at the thrill of heaven drawing him into its eternal bliss. This wasn't the wish he'd whispered, but he wouldn't deny himself the pleasure she bestowed upon him.

Barrett surrendered and wrapped his hands in her hair, drawing her closer. She needed no other encouragement. With each kiss and stroke of her tongue, Barrett's trembles grew. Her tongue drew him deeper inside her mouth where she slowly slid him in and out. His hardness throbbed in need, and her strokes grew bolder. Her mouth demanded more each time she sucked him in deeper and harder. His moans vibrated through them the more his control slipped. But still, Gemma wanted more.

She needed Barrett more than she needed the blood coursing through her veins.

Her mouth tormented him with each bold stroke of her tongue. He wanted to close his eyes and bask in the glory of Gemma's love. Watching her was an aphrodisiac. His cock grew harder each time her lips drew him in and out, but when the tip of her tongue trailed a fire of need, he thought he might explode. Then she pulled him out and blew a soft breath against him and licked her lips, hungry for more, and Barrett could wait no longer. He needed to sheath himself inside and come undone while deep in her core, striking his mark upon her soul.

Barrett lifted Gemma off the ground. "Wrap your legs around my waist," he growled.

As she did so, his lips captured hers, and he tasted himself on her tongue. With one arm holding her to him, he pulled her hair, exposing her neck. His head dived to suck the sensitive skin. He trailed a path of kisses and inhaled the scent of Gemma's desires on the spot right behind her ear. The musky fragrance enflamed his senses.

"I assume you have never taken a moonlit swim either," Barrett whispered in her ear.

Gemma arched, brushing her breasts across Barrett's chest, causing her nipples to tighten harder. She wanted his mouth back on her neck, his kisses marking her with his passion. While he waited for her answer, Gemma grew impatient and pulled his head back to suckle at her neck.

At first, he granted her wish. However, the longer she didn't answer, the more demanding his kisses grew until he lightly bit her.

She moaned. "No."

Barrett chuckled. Oh, their marriage bed would never be a bore. "Another first to share."

Barrett walked them to the pond and slowly immersed them into the water. The warm evening took the chill off. However, neither of them would have noticed because of the heat consuming their souls. Once he submerged them in the water, he moved over to the stones positioned around the pond. When he sank down, Gemma gasped, clasping onto him tighter.

"Easy, love."

Gemma relaxed at Barrett's tone once she realized there was a place for him to sit. Then the passion consuming her took hold again. She needed him. She felt his hardness pressing against her core and reached down to touch him. Her body shook from the turbulent emotions Barrett brought forth with each kiss and caress.

Barrett reached down and joined Gemma's hand with his. Her hand trembled under his, and he slowed her strokes, trying to calm the need that strung her tight. The same need his body demanded for him to release. However, he wanted to savor Gemma and make this moment memorable for her. Not frenzied when they had the time to make it magical.

He released his hand and lifted her breast out of the water. Droplets of water dripped from her nipple. He bent his head, drew the sweet temptation between his lips, and sucked softly. His tongue stroked the bud into a tight cherry. He drew the other breast above the water and gave the other bud the same pleasure. Soft, slow licks. Back and forth he suckled her nipples with little bites. Gemma writhed on his lap. He smiled before he clamped down on the bud, sucking harder. Her hand tightened on his cock when he scraped his teeth against the puckered cherry.

Gemma realized Barrett was tormenting her on purpose and decided to seek her own revenge. The stroke of her hand on his cock slowed. Her thumb brushed across the tip and lightly pressed along its ridge for a brief second before returning to her slow torment. Another moan escaped his lips, and Gemma brushed his cock against her wetness, gliding it back and forth.

Barrett didn't know whether to chuckle at her teasing or to take Gemma in one swift stroke. His siren learned quickly, but she still had much to learn.

One hand slid down, and he brushed his thumb across her clit where she had just teased his cock. While his thumb stroked Gemma's passion higher, his finger plunged deep inside her.

Gemma gasped. "Barrett."

He slid in another finger and kept them still until she pressed herself down on them. Then he began his torture, slowly drawing them in and out. Her bud tightened under his thumb and her pussy clenched around his fingers, letting him know Gemma was spiraling out of control. As much as he enjoyed pleasuring her, he needed to be inside her.

Once again, Barrett made Gemma lose all sense of herself. All she felt was the power of them as one. With love engrained so deep in her soul, it made her feel complete for the first time in her life.

Barrett drew out Gemma's desire until she thought she would lose her mind. He demanded more and more from her. What she gave him was never enough. Gemma kept discovering more about herself that she wanted to give him.

And Barrett wasn't a selfish lover who only took. No. He gave himself over to Gemma in the same manner, with a love more powerful than she ever imagined.

Gemma stilled and drew her hands up to his face. Her feather-light touch stroked over the rough bristles. She smiled, filled with love for him. Her lips found his. Soft. Slow. Gentle. Each kiss telling its own story of love.

Barrett slid inside Gemma, making them one. Their bodies matched the kisses passing between their lips. Soft. Slow. Gentle. Each stroke telling its own story of love. They tightened their grips around each other, their bodies arching with each thrust. Their lips never parted, only drawing away from each other to breathe. Barrett took them to the paradise their bodies craved, floating with the utter bliss of completion.

Barrett gazed into Gemma's eyes, watching her love transform into an emotion stronger than what they would ever understand. Love was too tame of a word for the emotion that consumed them. Yet, they needed to speak them.

"I love you, Gemma, more than I thought possible," he whispered.

"You hold my heart in your hands, Barrett. Please never drop it."

"I shall guard it next to mine forever." He sealed his promise with a kiss.

Chapter Sixteen

Susanna huffed. "Theo, I think you have allowed Gemma too much leniency. We are no longer at your estate in the country where the girls can sneak away and no one takes notice of their behavior. We are in the middle of London, where there are eyes everywhere."

Theo patted his sister-in-law's hand as they watched Ralston sneak Gemma into the secret passageway. It was the early hours of dawn. Soon the household would run afoot, preparing for their dinner this evening.

Susanna, like Theo, was an early riser. When Susanna joined him in his study, he had informed her of the events that had led to Ralston stealing Gemma away in the night. While Susanna fretted over how this would lead to the biggest scandal in London history, Theo relaxed back in his chair, grinning from ear to ear. He thought it quite romantic, the way Ralston carried Gemma through the garden and into his carriage. He supposed Gemma got her romantic nature from him. And it pleased him greatly that Ralston gifted Gemma with romantic overtures.

"Never fear, my dear. By the end of our dinner this evening, Gemma shall be engaged."

"To which gentleman?" Susanna raised an eyebrow. "Worthington or Ralston?"

"That will depend on how each gentleman reacts."

Susanna twisted her hands together. "But we did not invite Lord Ralston to dinner."

Colebourne grinned. "Yes, but that will not stop the marquess from coming. In fact, I know this is late notice, but please invite his parents, the Duke and Duchess of Theron, to dinner. I imagine the duchess will find the evening entertaining and they shall not refuse."

"I am switching my loyalty to Lucas." Susanna gave him a pointed look. "You have gone beyond mad, dipping into senile. Soon, someone will catch Gemma's indiscretions. She steals away with Ralston every time he dangles temptation in front of her. Then any chance we have at finding grooms for Jacqueline and Abigail shall be impossible."

Colebourne's smile widened. "We will not need to search for their grooms. Those two girls have already given their hearts to the gentleman of their choosing. We only need to guide them into the match."

"And Duncan?" Susanna narrowed her gaze.

"Already into play, my dear. In fact, I think after I have Gemma settled, we shall work on his union next."

"One that will rock the very foundation of this family."

Theo laughed. "That it shall."

Susana shook her head. On her way out the door, she kept muttering, "Mad, mad, mad."

Theo only laughed harder as he turned in his chair to watch the sun rise over the luscious blooms in his garden.

~~~~~

Selina stepped out of the grand dining room. Lady Forrester had invited Selina to help her prepare for the family dinner this evening since Selina needed to learn how the duke preferred his meals. She was to wed Lucas soon after all.

Her father and the duke had finally agreed the wedding would take place this fall at Colebourne's estate. The duke planned to announce the wedding date this evening.

She'd prepared herself for Lady Forrester's standoffish manner. Instead, the lady embraced Selina upon arrival and offered her kind advice, even allowing Selina to make her own personal touches on the dinner arrangement. Selina smiled at the warm acceptance. Ever since she sat next to the duke at the theatre, she'd started to relax in Colebourne's household. Perhaps her marriage to Lucas wouldn't be so awful after all.

Before she returned to her home to change, she wanted to give Gemma the letter she found. She still needed to warn Duncan, but she hadn't seen him since her arrival. Selina took the stairs to Gemma's bedroom. Outside the door, she wiped her palms down her skirts. With hesitation, she knocked softly on the door.

Gemma danced around her room, humming the same song Ralston had whispered in her ear during their dance in the garden at the Kanfold Ball. She floated across the floor, twirling in circles with happiness. A knock vibrated on the door, and she glided over to open it, expecting Abigail or Jacqueline.

Instead, Selina stood in the hallway. If there were ever a person to kill her mood, it was her cousin's intended. Gemma's smile slipped, and her guard rose. Even with Uncle Theo's lecture echoing in her head, she couldn't bring herself to treat Selina with anything but annoyance.

"Selina."

"Gemma. May I come in?"

Her uncle's reprimand kept repeating itself, so Gemma stepped back and swung her arm out, indicating for Selina to enter. She kept her bedroom door open, on the off chance someone would walk by and offer their support on dealing with the dragon.

Selina glanced around. "You have a lovely room."

"Thank you. What may I do for you?"

"We have never been friendly and I know I am partly to blame for the animosity between us."

Gemma didn't reply. Aunt Susanna always told them if they had nothing nice to say, then say nothing at all. It saved them from embarrassing themselves. Also, Gemma knew better than to trade barbs with Selina. Selina was too quick with her slander, while Gemma always avoided any trace of conflict. Usually, Charlie was the one to put Selina in her place. However, her cousin wasn't here, so Gemma must deal with Selina on her own.

When Gemma didn't respond to her, Selina realized it was hopeless to wish for things to miraculously change. No, she would have to show this family she harbored no ill feelings toward them. Which would take time.

Selina slipped her hand into her pocket and pulled out the letter she wanted to return. When she had retrieved the missive, it had lain in a crumpled mess. Selina had taken the time to smooth the letter and fold it neatly. She offered it over to Gemma as a token of friendship. However, Gemma misconstrued her gesture.

Gemma took the letter from Selina and realized it was the one she had lost at the theatre. The one where Ralston confessed his love and asked for her to trust him. In her cruelty to Abigail, she had forgotten the letter. Her eyes grew wide when she realized who held her secrets in the palm of her hand. She grabbed the letter and held it to her heart.

"How will you seek your revenge? Do you plan to expose my trysts with Ralston at dinner this evening?" Gemma's voice rose into a high pitch.

"No. No." Selina shook her head in denial.

"Then what do you want for your secrecy?"

"Nothing. I only wished to return what I found. Nothing more, but to warn you."

"Warn me you will hold this secret over my head for a lifetime!" Gemma shrieked.

Duncan flew into the room at the end of her accusation and immediately saw the reason for her distress. "Why can you not keep your spite to yourself?" he growled. "Do you have to strike your terror on everyone in your path?"

Selina raised her chin. "I only returned an item to your cousin and wanted to offer her—"

"Please spare the dramatics, *Duchess*," snarled Duncan.

A tear slipped from Selina's eye, and she furiously wiped it away. On her way to the door, she stopped in front of Gemma, trying to hide the hurt from her gaze, but failed. Unfortunately, an offer of kindness led to the same hatefulness. She still tried to warn Gemma.

"Please heed my warning. There is another person out to destroy your relationship with Lord Ralston and bring destruction to your family. Protect yourself and be honest with your uncle before it is too late," Selina whispered low enough so Duncan wouldn't hear.

Selina tore out of the room before anyone saw her crying, her tears falling faster than her steps. However, Duncan followed quickly on her heels and swung her around as she reached the bottom of the stairs. She tried wrenching out of his grasp, but his fingers dug into her arm. She kept her head lowered so he wouldn't see her tears. Before he started his lecture, the duke opened his study and noted Duncan clenching Selina.

"Duncan!" the duke roared. "Unhand Lady Selina."

Duncan blanched. "Uncle, you do not understand. Selina is terrorizing Gemma with her threats. She needs to realize our family will not welcome her malice."

"I did no such thing!" Selina wailed.

Colebourne noticed the tears falling along Lady Selina's cheeks and his nephew's brutal treatment of the miss. Perhaps he had misjudged this match and needed to devise a different plan for Lady Selina. It was the least he owed her for the mistreatment his family had subjected her to.

"Duncan, go take a ride!" Colebourne bellowed. Then his voice softened. "Lady Selina, please join me in my study while they bring your carriage around. I must apologize for my nephew's manners."

Selina nodded, pulling away from Duncan. Her heart ached at his callous disregard. His harsh comments opened her eyes to the fact that while they may share an undeniable attraction, he didn't think too highly of her character.

She followed the duke into his study. If Duncan wouldn't believe her innocence with Gemma, then he wouldn't believe the threat from Lady Langdale. She would need to confess the deception to Colebourne. The duke would understand the dilemma better than her own father and know how to proceed with the widow.

Selina walked into the duke's study. Lady Forrester stood just inside the room. The lady opened her arms wide for Selina as a mother would, and Selina walked into them, bawling like an undignified lady. She blabbered her sorrows and confessed everything on her mind. Her blush grew when she admitted to the kisses she'd shared with Duncan. But instead of shame,

Colebourne and Lady Forrester only offered her sympathy and understanding. The duke reassured Selina that he would deal with Lady Langdale and pleaded with her not to give up on hope for her future. The two convinced Selina to go home and pamper herself for the afternoon.

With a heavy heart, she left and wished she didn't have to return later. However, her entire life she'd never had a choice. She must learn to accept it.

Chapter Seventeen

Ralston hurried down the stairs, hoping to go undetected. He'd arrived early, before his mother awakened, and surprised his sisters by eating breakfast with them in the nursery. They'd squealed their delight and bombarded him with questions. Their nanny had made her displeasure clear with her pinched expression. She thought him a horrible influence because of the rumors circulating about his exploits. Ralston tried to charm her, but she refused to fall for his false compliments.

Now, the maids were a different story. They fawned over him and praised him for spending time with his sisters.

Before he left, his sisters wanted him to tell a story. They curled up on the sofa, and Ralston told them a tale about a mere mortal following in love with a siren. A make-believe story that had elements of his courtship with Gemma. They *ooh*ed and *aw*ed throughout the tale. They expressed their wishes of meeting the siren one day. He winked at them, promising them they stood a chance of making their wishes come true. Ralston took his leave after he had the girls well excited and unable to sit still. He chuckled, remembering the glare he'd received from the nanny.

His parents' quarrel echoed along the hallway when he reached the foyer. Only a few more steps and he would be in the clear.

However, the butler blocked his exit. "Lord Ralston, your parents have learned of your visit and request your presence before you leave."

Ralston cringed, knowing he would be met with a lecture. "Lead the way."

Ralston followed behind the butler, listening to his parents' passionate exchange. The servants tried to find a task nearby to listen as well. The butler motioned for them to return to work. When they reached his father's study, the butler stepped inside to announce him.

"I shall take it from here," Ralston mumbled.

The butler nodded, clearly relieved he didn't have to interrupt the duke and duchess. Ralston leaned against the doorjamb, waiting for his parents to acknowledge him. However, they were too deep in their discussion to notice. When they mentioned his name along with Gemma's, his ears perked up. He stepped into the room and cleared his throat, making his presence known. His father stopped pacing and his mother turned in surprise with her hands flittering in the air.

She came swiftly to his side, bussing his cheek. "What a delight, dear. Did you enjoy your visit with your sisters?"

"Yes, they are a charming pair. You have risen early, Mother."

"Yes. I have refrained from social events for a spell. Early to bed, early to rise, so they say."

Ralston frowned. "Are you ill?"

"No. She has finally placed the importance of her priorities in order," Ralston's father growled.

"Mmm. Then no more …"

"Your mother has promised to stop gambling and focus on her children."

Ralston breathed a sigh of relief at this news. Now he could concentrate on his work with Worth, instead of bailing his mother out from every gambling loss she accrued. It would appear his father had learned of his mother's debt and curbed her corrupt habits.

"All of her children," his father emphasized.

Ralston laughed. "I am more than capable of handling my own affairs."

"Are you?" he taunted.

"Yes," Ralston growled.

His father crossed his arms and pinned Ralston with his stare. "I disagree. You seem to have your hands full this season. With one unscrupulous widow and one very innocent debutante. Not to mention the debt you owe to Colebourne because of the same affliction you share with your mother. Why does Colebourne hold your vowels?"

Ralston tilted his head. "Mother, would you like to field this question?"

His father's gaze swung to his wife. "Duchess, you did not have Ralston claim your vowels?"

The duchess cringed, sitting down in defeat. "Perhaps."

"Is Colebourne blackmailing you? Is this the reason for your dalliances with his niece? Do you have to marry the chit to settle your mother's debts?" the duke demanded.

"I wish it were that simple. But to answer you, no. I am forbidden to have any contact with Gemma," he answered forlornly.

The duke frowned. "Then how are you clearing the debt?"

"I am to obtain a coin from the widow Langdale that her husband stole from Colebourne's family."

The duke narrowed his gaze. "That explains your inner action with Lady Langdale. However, it does not explain you sneaking around with the debutante."

The duchess shook her head in disappointment. "The ton is whispering, Ralston. There are rumors of occasions where you have spent time alone with her. I saw for myself at the Kanfold Ball."

Ralston sighed and slumped into a chair.

"You must make right by the girl. Either stay away from her or request her hand in marriage," the duke demanded.

"I plan to this evening. After I return the coin to Colebourne, I will ask him for his permission to marry Gemma."

"Do you love the girl?" asked his mother.

Ralston smiled. "Yes."

The duchess gasped. "Oh, how excellent."

The duke waved him away. "Then why are you still sitting here? Go get the damn coin, boy."

Ralston rose and glared at his father. He kissed his mother on the cheek. "I am pleased you have stopped gambling."

His mother ignored the comment. "Good luck with the girl. She is a beauty. Your father and I cannot wait to meet her."

Ralston nodded and left. When they were alone, the duchess turned to her husband. "Do you think we should have told him of our invite to Colebourne's dinner party this evening?"

The duke smirked. "Absolutely not. In fact, I think we shall arrive early and clear your gambling debt with Colebourne. Then once Barrett returns the coin to the duke, it shall only make him appear more worthy of the girl's hand."

"An excellent idea. I knew there was a reason I married you."

The duke drew the duchess into his arms. "The only reason?"

She laughed. "There might be more. Perhaps you can remind me of them."

The duke whispered the reasons in the duchess's ear and reminded her with kisses.

"Oh, now I recall." She sighed.

~~~~~~~

"Lucas looks most fierce this evening. Does he not?" Gemma asked Abigail and Duncan.

Lucas was scowling with Lady Selina by his side. They were conversing with Uncle Theo and Selina's father.

"It is because the duke plans to announce Lucas and Selina's wedding date during dinner. I overheard Lucas arguing with Uncle Theo before the guests arrived," Duncan growled.

"Oh, Abigail." Gemma reached for Abigail's hand.

Abigail shook her head. She clearly didn't want any special attention directed toward her. Gemma noticed the tears her friend tried to keep at bay and understood that any sign of comfort would cause her distress, but she only wanted to offer her friend support.

"Give me any sign and we shall sneak away."

Abigail drew in a deep breath. "I am fine. I knew this day would come soon. Now, please explain the fuss with Selina this afternoon. I meant to question you earlier, but Aunt Susanna needed my help."

"Yes, what did she want with you?" Duncan growled, shooting daggers at Selina.

"Nothing."

Gemma had mistaken Selina's intent earlier in the day. Her defensive guard had prompted her to strike without giving Selina the benefit of the doubt. While she assumed the worst, Selina's visit was the complete opposite. Selina never threatened her. In fact, she'd given her a warning.

However, she didn't know who Selina had warned her about. She hoped to speak with her before dinner, but no opportunity had presented itself. Selina had offered kindness, and Gemma threw it back in her face. Selina could have used the letter as a threat, but she hadn't.

"It was not nothing? You were screaming at her like a banshee," said Duncan.

Gemma shook her head. "It was only a misunderstanding."

Abigail gave her a strange look. "What kind of misunderstanding?"

Gemma glanced at Selina. "She returned an item I lost, 'tis all."

Duncan crossed his arms, still not swayed. "With threats?"

"No, with a warning."

"She has gone too far." Duncan twisted to move toward Selina.

"No," Gemma whispered. "She warned me of someone wishing to harm me and to be careful."

"Who?"

Gemma shrugged. "You did not give a chance before you ran her off."

"She was kind to you?" Abigail asked in disbelief.

"Yes." Gemma bit her lip. "But I was cruel to her."

Duncan shook his head. "I do not believe it."

"Well, believe it. 'Tis the truth."

"Humph." Duncan mumbled more about ladies' behaviors before sauntering away.

"Do you owe her an apology?" inquired Abigail.

Gemma nodded. "Yes."

"Now is the perfect time." Abigail pointed at Selina.

Selina stood by herself for the first time since she'd arrived. She was near the balcony doors with her gaze focused on the rug.

Gemma excused herself from Abigail and walked over to Selina. "Selina?"

Selina raised her head and glanced nervously around her. Her gaze traveled over to Duncan, then to Lucas before looking at Gemma. "Gemma."

"I want to apologize for my behavior earlier today."

Selina narrowed her gaze. "Is your uncle making you apologize?"

"No. Why would he?"

"Ahh. No reason." Selina's gaze flittered away again.

Gemma frowned. "Did you tell him what I said to you?"

Selina sighed. "Only because he made me confess why Duncan held onto me."

"Duncan held you?" Gemma asked in surprise.

"No. He only held onto my arm. That was all."

"Oh." Gemma glanced over at Duncan and noticed he was staring at Selina with a purpose. When she looked at Selina, she saw her gaze kept straying toward Duncan. "Ohhh."

"What?" asked Selina.

Gemma smiled. She wanted to laugh, but it would have to wait until later. She couldn't wait to share her suspicions with Abigail. Gemma didn't believe it was possible, but it had to be. She remembered Charlie had shared a secret with Duncan that involved Selina. This must be the secret.

"Nothing. I just remembered something I forgot to take care of."

Selina attempted a smile but failed. Gemma noticed the distress in the girl's eyes. Had Gemma and her cousins misjudged Selina all these years? Was Uncle Theo correct in Selina's character? If so, they'd paid the girl a grand injustice all along. They had much to make up for. Now that

Gemma recalled, she never saw Selina surrounded by any friends. Only her father.

"Thank you for returning my letter. I am sorry for treating you so harshly."

Gemma prepared herself for an insult or a sarcastic comment. However, Selina said nothing at all, merely nodded. She appeared worn down, as if she had lost all interest in fighting. The silence felt awkward, yet Gemma didn't want to leave Selina's side.

A strange idea bloomed. Could they be friends? She could hear her family's shocked comments once they learned of her intentions. Still, she wanted to try.

"There is a rumor floating around that Uncle Theo plans to announce your wedding date during dinner. You must be excited."

"Mmm, yes. Thrilled." Selina transformed before her very eyes. She pasted on a brittle smile, trying to appear serene.

Gemma laughed. She shouldn't have. However, Gemma believed that if your eyes didn't convey the same story of happiness you tried to portray, then you portrayed a falsity. Selina's eyes spoke of her aversion to marrying Lucas.

Gemma arched a brow. "Really?"

"Why would I not be?"

"Oh, maybe because you hold feelings for my other cousin." Gemma nodded her head toward Duncan.

Selina paled. "You know?" she whispered.

"I only guessed."

"Oh, no. No." Selina twisted her head to see if anyone had heard. She wrung her hands repeatedly in front of her.

Gemma drew Selina outdoors and walked them away from any prying ears. "Calm down. Your secret is safe with me. You hold my secret, now I hold yours. Why do you not have your father call off the betrothal?"

Selina shook her head frantically. "I cannot. Father has anticipated my marriage to Lord Gray my entire life. Every day, he has drilled into me what my duty is to our family. It does not matter anyway. Duncan Forrester is a Scottish heathen who only trifles with me for his amusement. He holds no feelings for me. If I break the betrothal and Duncan refuses to ask for my hand, no gentleman will."

"Uncle Theo will make Duncan," Gemma assured Selina.

"Having my marriage arranged with Lucas is a longstanding tradition with peers. However, I have no wish to have a man forced to marry me." Selina sighed. "While I long for love, I would welcome a friendship with Lucas versus resentment if your uncle had to force Duncan."

Gemma nodded. "I understand."

Selina didn't speak immediately. After a moment, she told Gemma, "I hope you find happiness with Lord Ralston."

"We will. I have not been friendly in the past, but I wish to change that. I hope you will accept my offer of friendship from this day forth."

Selina gifted her with a tentative smile. "Thank you."

"Before we go back inside, can you explain what you meant about an enemy?"

"Lady Langdale means to seek revenge against your family, and she has chosen you as her target."

Gemma stared at Selina, confused. "I do not understand."

Selina bit her lip. "She is furious Lord Worthington threw her over for Evelyn and how Lord Ralston's interest lies in your direction. You must watch your back."

Before Gemma could respond, Aunt Susanna came to the door and urged them inside. Goodwin had announced dinner, and they needed to rejoin the party.

Selina smiled at her and followed Aunt Susanna indoors. Gemma paused and contemplated what Selina had said. She needed to discuss this information with Ralston. However, she didn't know where to find him.

But Worth did.

~~~~~~

Ralston took a slug from his flask. He needed the liquid courage to deal with the widow. He'd drunk half a bottle of whiskey before he left. Ralston might have had one too many. But the thought of kissing, let alone touching, Lady Langdale twisted his stomach into knots. He hoped the plan he'd put together with Worth worked. Because he couldn't bed the widow. No. He refused to.

He strode up the stairs to Lady Langdale's townhome. The door stood open, and the servants scurried around with trunks and hat boxes. He looked around, wondering what was happening. When he tried to inquire, all he learned was that the widow had prepared for a trip. A trip to where?

He heard Lady Langdale giving orders above him, and he took the stairs two at a time to reach her. Barbara stood in her bedroom with clothes strewn everywhere. Her maid was filling a trunk near the bed.

"Going somewhere?"

Barbara jumped at his voice. She turned and pretended surprise at his appearance, even though they had made plans for dinner. She fluttered her hand at her maid to leave. With a seductive smile, she glided to his side.

The widow ran her hand down his front. Before she reached his trousers, he clamped his hand around her wrist. He tried not to cringe, but he had no control over how his body reacted. Barbara noticed and snarled at him, shaking off his grip.

She sauntered away, resuming her packing. "As a matter of fact, I am."

"May I ask where to?"

"The continent."

"What of our deal?" he growled.

Barbara rolled her eyes. "Our deal is void, Lord Ralston."

"May I still purchase the coin from you?"

Barbara laughed, shaking her head. "No."

"Why not?" Ralston asked.

When she refused to answer him, Ralston stalked to her side and turned her around. He gripped her arms and asked her again about the coin.

"I no longer hold the coin in my possession." Her smile was full of vindictive pleasure.

Ralston stilled, his eyes widening. He hadn't anticipated her selling it. "Who holds it now?"

"The Duke of Colebourne. Who else?"

Ralston narrowed his eyes. "I do not understand."

Barbara huffed. "What is there to understand?"

"We had a deal."

She tried to shake off his hold. "A deal that you reengaged on with your infatuation with another."

"What infatuation?"

"Gemma Holbrooke," she gritted between her teeth.

Ralston loosened his grip, stroking his hands along her arms. He lifted his hand and ran his knuckle across the widow's cheek. He watched her eyes cloud with desire and leaned in to whisper in her ear. "I only dallied with her to play with her emotions. To lure her into our trap of revenge. Once I had her smitten with desire, I have ignored her."

Barbara pulled back. "I saw you kiss her at the Kanfold Ball. She was not the only one smitten."

"A trick to draw attention to her absence." Ralston shrugged as if it were no big deal. "I hoped to cause whispers of how easy the girl was to seduce."

"There were no whispers to overhear."

Ralston sighed. "Yes. Her family is very powerful on that front, I realized to my dismay."

"You lie, Lord Ralston."

"Nonsense," Ralston denied, trailing his finger along her neck and across her heaving bosom.

"Prove it and kiss me," Barbara challenged.

"I have nothing to prove anymore. Your actions have ruined any chance for my protection. You double-crossed me." Ralston pushed her away from him.

His thoughts were frantic on how to proceed. Without the coin, they couldn't turn her over to the authorities. His and Worth's relentless dedication over the last year had been for naught. Not to mention his standing with Colebourne on returning his family's prized possession was ruined. How would he convince the duke to allow him to court Gemma now?

Barbara rubbed her arms, easing the pain from his grip. "Please. You were the one who did not fill his part of the bargain. You promised an affair this season in exchange for the coin, so I would not be subjected to ridicule after Worthington threw me over for his bride. Instead, you became involved with the cousin, making a mockery of the relationship I tried to convince the ton of. Not to mention the offer of protection from my late husband's nefarious activities. Once I realized I stood alone in my quest to reaffirm my standing in society, I took matters upon myself to handle. I returned the coin to Colebourne, pleading my innocence. I've decided to visit the continent. This season is tedious, and I grow weary of the glances of pity directed my way. I may extend my visit for a couple of years until the rumors of Worthington's rejection fade."

Ralston needed to find Worth. They needed to figure out how to stop the widow from leaving town. His time here was over. He no longer needed to pretend an interest in the lovely widow. He was free to pursue Gemma. Colebourne remained the only obstacle to overcome. Since his father knew of his mother's gambling habit, he would pay off her debt with the duke.

He didn't bother turning to make his departure known. While Lady Langdale remained a priority, she wasn't the one he wanted to focus his attention on. It would take her a couple of days to settle her affairs before she left the country. Which would leave them plenty of time to trap her. Now, he only wanted to plead his case to Colebourne.

When he strode to the door and threw it open, Lady Langdale laughed. "I do hope you are not in a hurry to win Lady Gemma's hand."

Ralston paused with his hand on the doorknob and turned slowly. Once he faced the widow, he arched his eyebrow at her, not saying a word.

She glanced at the clock, a cunning smile lighting her face. "By now she is engaged to Mr. Worthington."

"Why do you believe Gemma and Worth are engaged?" he growled.

Her smile widened. "Why, a little birdie might have whispered in the duke's ear of a rendezvous they shared earlier this week. When I returned the coin, the duke confirmed their engagement and asked for my silence. Of course, I agreed. However, since their family dinner is almost finished, I believe the secret is safe to tell. To you, at least. But then you are the only one I wish to share the gossip with."

Ralston scowled. "Do you not mean I am the only one you wish to rub it in my face?"

Lady Langdale continued to laugh with glee. With a glare in her direction, he left in a hurry. Ralston heard the clock strike, announcing the hour. On his way outside, he listened to the last stroke of eight. He hoped there was still time to stop the duke from announcing Gemma and Worth's engagement. The widow's laughter echoed off the walls and continued to follow him to his carriage. The cackle set his emotions on edge, and he cursed his failures during the ride to Colebourne's home.

He'd failed to prevent Gemma's engagement to his friend. He'd failed to bring the illustrious widow to justice. Not only was the love of his life engaged to his friend, but he also risked his relationship with Worth.

Because Worth's fury at not securing Lady Langdale's confession could be the end of their business, not to mention their friendship.

Chapter Eighteen

It pleased Gemma when Aunt Susanna sat Worth to her right during dinner. However, she sat Duncan on her left. Before she could ask Worth to deliver a message to Ralston, Duncan started lecturing her for talking to Selina alone. He had worked himself into a state of agitation over her new friend. As much as she wished to talk to Worth, she found too much amusement with Duncan.

She smiled at him while he ranted. Her amused state went unnoticed because he kept his scrutiny focused on Selina. At first, he muttered at Selina's motives for revenge, then he switched to his opinion of her character, calling her a minx, a seductive goddess, then back to calling her a viper.

Gemma noticed Selina was trying to avoid his glare, but she kept glancing their way. Selina appeared unaffected by Duncan, but her eyes gave her away. Their depths were filled with a hurt so profound, guilt settled over Gemma at the part she'd played in Selina's loneliness. In the past, she'd have thought the expression was one of disdain. Now she realized Selina's coldness was because she protected herself from the cruelty Gemma's family directed at her.

Soon shame consumed her, intensifying the guilt. A loving family had surrounded Gemma her entire life. Her own parents had displayed their love at every opportunity. Once they passed, her uncle and cousins had continued with the same affection. Uncle Theo even encouraged her fanciful infatuations with romance and everlasting love. Never in her cocoon of acceptance and happiness did she realize not everyone held the same security in their lives. Selina was under the belief that her only purpose was to please others, never herself.

Now, with her eyes wide open, Gemma planned to right the wrongs of her family. Perhaps with a little push of encouragement, Gemma could convince Duncan to pursue Selina.

"Please stop with your utter ramblings. You do not fool me for one instance, Duncan Forrester."

Duncan swung his gaze from Selina and focused on Gemma. He narrowed his eyes and glared at her. "Pardon me?"

Gemma laughed and leaned close to him, whispering, "I know your secret."

"What secret?" Duncan growled.

"It is perfectly safe with me. I even promised Selina to keep quiet on her feelings regarding you."

"I have no …" Duncan glanced around them to see if anyone was paying attention. "Selina holds feelings toward me?" he murmured.

Gemma shrugged before turning her attention toward Worth once she noticed he wasn't talking with anyone. She engaged Worth in polite conversation before she attempted to discuss Ralston with him. She'd planted questions in Duncan's head about Selina, so he could stew over her comments. Duncan kept trying to gain her attention back, but she ignored him. He went so far as to tug at her dress and pinch her arm. Gemma wanted to laugh at his dilemma, but she needed to address her own problems first. However, before she asked Worth of Ralston's whereabouts, he asked her a question she herself wondered.

"Do you know why your uncle invited Ralston's parents to dinner?"

Gemma bit her lip. "I do not know. I thought this to only be a family dinner."

Worth narrowed his gaze at Colebourne. "If so, why invite the entire Worthington clan? From rumors circulating, he plans to announce the date for Lady Selina and Gray's wedding."

Gemma shrugged. "With Evelyn's marriage to Reese, he now considers your entire family one with ours."

"Hmm." Worth pursed his lips. "That still does not explain why Ralston's parents are present."

Gemma took a sip of wine. "I am sure Uncle Theo has his reasons. However, since they are here, where is Ralston?"

Worth shrugged. "Perhaps Ralston had another engagement that captured his attention."

"Do you know where that might be?"

Worth looked everywhere but at Gemma. He appeared uncomfortable with her question, even making a comment across the table to engage with their conversation. But when that conversation ended, he faltered at his attempt to engage Jaqueline on his other side. Which left him at Gemma's mercy.

"Where is he?" she repeated. "I must speak to him."

"And how do you attempt to find him?"

"With your help." Gemma gave Worth her most dazzling smile that fell flat at his frown and the shake of his head. "Please."

Worth shook his head again. "Absolutely not."

"Why not?"

Worth sighed. "Because you would be unwelcome company." When Gemma looked at him with confusion, he offered, "I can pass him a message."

"Who is he with?" Gemma hissed.

"Gemma, let it lie for the night. I promise Ralston will call on you when he can."

"Who? Where?" Gemma demanded.

Worth looked to the ceiling for answers. He and Ralston were so near to the end of finishing their assignment. Tonight should draw their hard work over the last year to a close. After Ralston gained the coin and gathered Lady Langdale's implication in the thievery ring, his friend could live happily ever after.

To secure Ralston's actions, he must stop Gemma from going after him.

"He is spending the evening in Lady Langdale's arms."

"You are lying." But Gemma's voice wavered.

Worth turned to her with an expression he used to bluff gentleman into pushing all their blunt into the pot to beat him. The look never failed him to achieve his goals. And his goal this evening was to secure his future. No amount of friendship with Gemma Holbrooke would stop him.

Worth cocked an eyebrow. "Am I?"

Gemma's eyes widened at his blunt stare. When tears filled her eyes, it confirmed her belief. He had accomplished his goal for now. However, Gemma was persistent, and she wouldn't believe in his lie for long.

Before she could continue with her questions, the Duke of Colebourne saved him from any further interrogation when he clinked a knife against a wine glass. "If I could have everyone's attention."

The table grew quiet, the guests focusing their attention on her uncle. The expressions were a mixture of curiosity and dread. Gemma set her own problems to the side for now. She didn't feel heartache but annoyance at Worth for lying to her about Ralston's whereabouts. Gemma believed there were no rooms for lies in their friendship, but obviously Worth felt differently.

"I have invited everyone here to make two announcements. The first, I am sure you gather, is the long-awaited wedding date for my son. With much discussion, Norbury and I have decided on a date for the nuptials."

Colebourne paused for a dramatic effect. Selina and Lucas rose at this declaration. However, the table remained silent. She wished her family held a different opinion of Selina and didn't look at Uncle Theo with trepidation. Ironically, she'd felt the same way about Selina only hours before. Yet, her feelings had changed, and she needed to show her support for Selina.

He shook his head at the family. "The wedding shall take place on the third Saturday of September this year at my estate. After many years of waiting, Lucas and Selina shall become bride and groom. Husband and wife. So from our family to yours, welcome, Lady Selina. We hope you enjoy our family as much as we enjoy you."

Colebourne toasted Selina, smiling his welcome to their family. A preliminary gesture, but one that would be final in a couple of months. Selina's lips lifted in a serene smile, and a blush graced her cheeks. When the table still sat quietly, with no one offering their well-wishes, Colebourne nudged Lucas.

With a frown, Lucas lifted his glass in Selina's direction. "A day I am anxiously awaiting. To Lady Selina." He drained his glass.

Selina's smile slipped away at Lucas's lack of enthusiasm.

Gemma pushed her chair back to welcome Selina into their family with warm affection. She rounded the table and wrapped her in a hug. "Keep smiling," Gemma whispered in Selina's ear before she pulled away.

Selina pasted her smile back on and lifted her chin. Gemma smiled in approval and encouragement. As her gaze trailed around the table, her family looked back at her in shock at her kind gesture. Abigail's mouth hung wide open, Charlie's eyes narrowed, and Evelyn and Jacqueline held bewildered expressions. Tomorrow morning, they would no doubt invade her room for a full explanation. For now, they remembered their manners and Uncle Theo's threat by offering the couple their congratulations.

Once everyone returned to their seats, Uncle Theo asked Gemma to remain standing. Then to further confuse her, he also asked Worth to rise too.

"Lady Worthington, you might be wondering why I have invited your family to such an intimate gathering. And my answer to you is that it only seemed fitting to announce Gemma's engagement to Worth in your presence. I am delighted to bring our families even closer with their happy union. However, there is a need to rush the arrangement for this wedding. But nothing a special license will not help matters along."

Gemma didn't need to see her reflection to know she'd paled at her uncle's words. Why would he make such an announcement? When she hazarded a glance at Worth, he looked furious at Uncle Theo's trap. His hands curled into fists at his sides. The table erupted into a million questions. Every question wondered from a secret courtship to why they hid their attachment.

"Quiet, quiet. I shall explain myself," Colebourne said with authority. "A peer has brought to my attention of seeing Gemma and Worth in questionable sightings. Alone," Colebourne added.

Lady Worthington gasped. "Is this true?"

Noel jumped in. "No, Mama. It is not. I can vouch for—"

"That is enough, Noel," Worth interrupted her.

Noel huffed in frustration. "But—"

"Noel, please stay quiet. This does not concern you," Reese Worthington said firmly, then swung his gaze to his younger brother. "I warned you to stay away from Gemma. You never listen. Yet another mess you have created that I must clean up."

Gemma stood in shock, not able to declare Worth's innocence. She couldn't believe her uncle had trapped them into one of his matchmaking schemes. It was an outcome she didn't expect, nor would she accept. She couldn't believe the reaction Worth was receiving from his family. Their disappointment was clear, and he didn't deserve it.

Uncle Theo returned to his seat while the verbal slander passed back and forth. A conniving smile graced his face and amusement lit his eyes at the chaos. He took pleasure from his announcements. Oh, the man was maddening. And Gemma refused to stand for it. However, before she declared her intentions, the door to the dining room swung open.

Ralston stormed into the room, followed by a bevy of footmen trying to stop him. Finally, they could make sense of the mess her uncle had created.

Uncle Theo grinned. "Ahh, Lord Ralston, you are just in time for the toast congratulating Mr. Worthington and Gemma's engagement announcement. Goodwin, please get Lord Ralston a glass of champagne."

"Like hell," Ralston snarled.

"Language, Lord Ralston. There are ladies present, your mother included," reprimanded Colebourne with a smirk.

Ralston's nostrils flared in anger. "Gemma is not marrying Worth."

Colebourne's smug smile grew wider. "You have no choice in the matter."

"I have every choice in the matter."

"Ralston! Now is not the time for this discussion," his father growled.

Ralston swung his head to his father. "Why are you here?"

"His Grace sent us an invitation. However, I am most confused as to why since this appears to be a family celebration," Ralston's mother replied.

"Do you wish to know why, Mother?" Ralston ground his teeth. "Colebourne considers this a game. We are nothing but pawns for his amusement. He moves each of us to his advantage, sparing no one an opportunity to make a move guaranteeing their own happiness."

Colebourne chuckled lightly. "Such harsh words, my boy. When, in fact, I have allowed you many moves on your own. However, your participation in the game has only brought about the ruination of my niece with each play."

Ralston tightened his hands into fists at his side. "Only because you refused my offer to court Gemma because of a debt I owed. Then you dangled a chance to redeem myself. However, before I could, you withheld information that the offer had settled on its own. You left me to pursue a woman, watching and waiting to see if I would cross the line on the promises I made toward Gemma. Well, Your Grace, you failed at that attempt. And you will fail on forcing Worth and Gemma to wed."

"Will I?" Colebourne's tone was mild. "Since you were unable to fulfill your part of the bargain, it leaves your debt still held in my possession. And as long as you owe me, I cannot allow my niece to marry a reprobate who gambles away his fortune. Not to mention how scandal falls in your wake at every debutante or wife you dally with. I will not subject Gemma to a life of depravity."

"You did not gain the coin?" asked Worth.

"Later," Ralston snarled.

"No. Now." Worth pounded his fist on the table. "Because of your failure, I am now engaged and my family looks upon me with disapproval. You only had to accomplish one thing this evening, and you failed. Explain yourself."

Ralston shook his head. "When I arrived at Lady Langdale's townhome, I found her preparing for a trip to the continent. She informed me of how she had returned the coin to the duke and explained how she set her plan of revenge into motion. It was her intent to ruin the Worthington and Holbrooke family for the way Reese threw her over for Evelyn."

"She plans to leave? We must stop her." Worth grabbed at Ralston to drag him away.

Ralston shook him off. "She is in the early stages of packing. We still have time to trap her into a confession. Even without the coin, we have enough evidence to threaten her with the authorities."

"No, you are probably too late," interrupted Reese. "Lady Langdale has perfected the art of leaving town. She is long gone by now. In the past, she disappeared before I even realized she no longer remained in town."

Worth shook his head in defeat and slumped in the chair. "All our hard work has disappeared. Not closing this case has ruined us. No one will trust us again."

Reese stared at him with suspicion. "What hard work? Graham, what are you involved in?"

"It does not matter anymore. I suppose since I must now take a bride, I am going to need my allowance reinstated."

Ralston gritted his teeth. "I repeat, like hell you will wed Gemma."

"Barrett William Ralston, watch your language!" his mother yelled.

Colebourne chuckled at Her Grace's discipline. She swung her gaze to him, glaring. He closed his mouth and sat up straighter in his chair.

"And for shame, Colebourne. If Lady Langdale returned the coin, you owed Ralston an explanation instead of sending him into that shrew's den. Also, that debt was not to hold over Ralston's head. That was mine and is now clear. You accepted our payment before dinner. Therefore, you can no longer threaten him with that excuse."

Colebourne inclined his head. "Very true, Duchess. But I can deny him because he tempted Gemma into inappropriate incidents and then did not make his claim for her hand."

"Like the supposed sighting you tried to trap Worth into admitting to?" asked Lady Worthington. "Noel, please explain what you were about to say earlier."

Noel glanced at her brother in uncertainty. "Graham?"

Worth waved her on with a sigh. "It is all right. If you do not speak it, Ralston shall."

Noel nodded. "Gemma and Worth were not alone in the carriage. Lord Ralston and I were also with them. Worth and I took a walk while they were alo—"

Worth held up a hand. "You have said enough, Noel."

"No, my dear, please continue," ordered Colebourne.

Noel glanced around nervously. "Only that when we reached the cottage, Gemma and Ralston needed time alone to talk. So Graham and I took a stroll on a path behind the cottage," Noel rushed on with her explanation.

"Colebourne!" the duchess and Lady Worthington shouted.

Reese shook his head. "What I do not understand is this talk of confessions and your involvement in capturing Lady Langdale. And for what crime?"

Worth glanced at his brother. "Over the course of the past two years, Ralston and I have retrieved stolen items for peers of the ton. When Colebourne asked Ralston to retrieve a stolen coin from Lady Langdale, we knew this was our opportunity to display our status as private investigators to the ton. If we retrieved the coin, it would show they could trust us to settle any case they brought our way."

Worth paused, gauging his family's reaction. "When Bow Street heard of our endeavor, they asked for our help in stopping a thievery ring involving Lady Langdale. They knew of your past affair with the widow and wondered if we could help them. We only needed to retrieve the coin for Colebourne, and Ralston was to convince Lady Langdale to trust him with her secrets. However, my partner here went and fell in love, placing the case in jeopardy because he couldn't hide his infatuation. Now not only were we unable to return the coin to Colebourne, thereby showing the depth of our skills, but the confession has also slipped from our fingers with Lady Langdale's disappearance."

"Sorry, mate," Ralston muttered.

Worth waved his hand and lifted his glass, draining it in one swallow. He lifted it for the servant to refill.

"What if I could offer evidence to implicate Lady Langdale?" asked Colebourne.

Ralston focused on him. "What kind of proof do you hold?"

"A confession from her cohort. After their last caper, she double-crossed him and kept the loot for herself."

"Can we trust him?" asked Worth.

Colebourne nodded. "I would say we can. If you gentlemen will join me in my study, I believe we can make a deal. Once finished, we can join the ladies to finish celebrating my announcements."

"One of your announcements is false," muttered Ralston.

"So it is. In time, it shall change, but for now, it stands," declared Colebourne.

"Colebourne," Lady Worthington and the duchess warned.

Colebourne sighed dramatically. "Very well. I am calling off the engagement between Mr. Worthington and Gemma."

"And?" prompted Gemma.

Colebourne sighed dramatically again. "And after our discussion of Lady Langdale, I shall decide if Lord Ralston will make a suitable husband for you."

Gemma smirked. "Which you know he will."

Colebourne tried biting back a smile. "We shall see."

"Good luck," Jasper Sinclair, Charlie's husband, directed at Ralston.

"Another victim of the duke's mad matchmaking scheme," muttered Worthington.

"Excuse me? Can someone please explain?" asked Ralston.

"My father has taken it upon himself to play matchmaker where his wards are concerned. I am afraid you are his latest victim, Lord Ralston," explained Gray.

Gemma slipped her hand inside Ralston's and beamed at his side. "Do not worry, my dear. My uncle only likes to toy with others when they have bested him at his own game."

"So the rumors of madness are true?" asked Ralston.

Gemma smiled. "Yes."

Rumbles of laughter filled the dining room air.

Chapter Nineteen

Gemma visited with the duchess while she waited for Barrett and the other gentlemen to return. The duchess exclaimed her glee over Barrett finding a lady as charming as Gemma for a wife. Like all mothers, the duchess boasted his greater attributes. Gemma found amusement when the duchess portrayed Barrett as a proper gentleman, as her description was far from the truth. However, the longer the gentlemen stayed amongst themselves, the more Gemma feared Uncle Theo would deny Barrett's request for her hand in marriage.

Soon Aunt Susanna called the duchess over to join her and Lady Worthington to discuss the best choice of flowers to use for a late summer wedding. Gemma noticed Selina cringe at the plans for her upcoming wedding with Lucas. Selina's predicament saddened Gemma, but not as much as seeing her sitting alone. Even after Gemma's warm reception at dinner, her cousins still excluded Selina.

Gemma strolled across the room, settled on the settee next to Selina, and offered her a smile of reassurance. Selina returned her smile, but the gesture never reached her eyes. No, they still held a sadness Gemma wished to never experience. However, if her uncle insisted on a marriage to Worth, Gemma would hold a kinship with the beauty.

"Thank you," said Selina.

Gemma shook her head. "Whatever for?"

Selina gave her a small, sincere smile. "For the hug after your uncle's announcement. You were most generous with your affections."

"I meant what I said before. We are now friends and that is how friends treat each other."

Selina's eyes warmed at Gemma's declaration. "Then as your friend, my advice to you is to make your love known for Lord Ralston ring loud and clear."

Gemma's eyes twinkled. "Oh, I plan to. Can I tell you a secret?"

"Yes."

"Uncle Theo is a big softie underneath his heavy-handedness. He has a kind heart," whispered Gemma.

"So I have recently learned for myself."

"You have?"

Selina's gaze flittered around the room. "Yes. But I told him I would not speak of our conversation. He did offer me some advice. He said matters will soon sort themselves out in the end."

Gemma nodded seriously. "Then trust in him. You will not regret it."

"May I ask what your plans are?" asked Selina.

"Why, to outsmart Uncle Theo any way I can." Gemma laughed.

Selina laughed along with her, and soon the other young ladies joined them. They teased Gemma over her sudden engagement to Worth and Ralston's fury at learning about Uncle Theo's trickery. Each lady offered her advice on how to handle Uncle Theo. Gemma nodded and smiled. She didn't need any advice on dealing with Uncle Theo. She never had. Her uncle enjoyed Gemma's quick wit and took delight when she tried to outsmart him. She wouldn't need to use any maneuvers to convince Uncle

Theo. He only wished for Gemma to find love and happiness, and he would never deny her a lifetime with Barrett. That Gemma knew for certain.

Abigail was the only person Gemma wanted to hear advice from. As usual, Abigail made herself scarce. She'd snuck out of the drawing room while Gemma talked with Selina. To Abigail, it appeared as if Gemma had abandoned her lifelong friend for the known enemy. The ultimate betrayal.

Also, Uncle Theo's announcement of a wedding date for Lucas and Selina only made Abigail's despair deepen. Now Abigail must face that the love she held for Lucas would never bear fruition. Instead, it would wither and die.

Gemma had hoped to spend time with Barrett, but her greatest wish was denied. Goodwin delivered a note to Aunt Susanna, apologizing for the need to end the evening. The gentlemen had taken leave for parts unknown and informed the ladies to take the carriages home. When the hour grew later, the duchess, Selina, and the Worthington ladies thanked them for a lovely evening and left. Aunt Susanna bid them goodnight and retired to her bedroom. Which left Gemma alone with her cousins. They sat across from her, smirking at the predicament she had gotten herself into.

"Spill," Charlie demanded. "I want to hear why you have defected to the enemy's side."

"I must find Abigail," said Gemma.

She rose and continued to Abigail's bedroom where her friend was sleeping. Or she appeared asleep, but she didn't fool Gemma for one minute. While Abigail always presented herself as a proper lady, she slept like a wild animal. Blankets strewn all over the bed, pillows on the floor, her body sprawled across the bed. And she mumbled in her sleep. She was the most annoying bed partner if you had to share a bedroom with her. However, the bedcovers remained tucked into the corners, and Abigail lay as still as a book on a shelf.

"Gemma. Leave her be, she is asleep. Whatever you need to say to her can wait until tomorrow morning," insisted Jacqueline.

Gemma hmphed. "Nonsense. Abigail is not asleep. She only pretends."

Gemma strode through the bedroom and made herself comfortable on a chair. Evelyn glanced back and forth between Gemma and Abigail and with a sigh, entered the room, sitting on the chaise.

Charlie laughed and strolled into the bedroom, taking a seat next to Evelyn. She turned to Gemma and repeated her demand. She wanted all the details of Ralston and her new sudden friendship with Selina Pemberton.

Jaqueline relented and took a seat but told them to keep their conversation to a whisper. A reprimand they ignored, but they did talk softly so as not to draw the attention of Aunt Susanna down the hall.

Gemma explained about the misunderstanding with Selina yesterday, then repeated the conversation she'd had with Selina before dinner and her offer of friendship. As Gemma talked, she noticed Abigail shifting on the bed so she could watch Gemma talk.

"I believe all these years we have misunderstood Selina. My offer of friendship is not an act of betrayal to our friendship, Abby."

"Now it is more real. She will get to be his wife," choked Abigail.

"Oh, love." Gemma went to Abigail and drew her into her arms.

Abigail cried, and they tried to comfort her the best they could. Even though she spoke the truth, they tried to reassure her that it wasn't final. After Abigail calmed, they sprawled across the bed, each lost in their own thoughts of Abigail's future. Gemma hoped in time a miracle would happen and tear Lucas and Selina apart. Her wish was for all parties involved.

Soon, Gemma grew drowsy at the quietness.

"And Lord Ralston?" asked Charlie.

Gemma yawned. "That is simple."

"How so?" asked Evelyn.

"Uncle will see the error of his ways and grant us permission to marry. He will have no choice in the matter," Gemma murmured.

The bedroom took on the familiar sound of laughter and love. Gemma smiled, staring at the ceiling, comforted by their presence. She loved each person in this room and would miss their constant presence in her life. But as Charlie and Evelyn had proven since they got married, they were only a carriage ride away.

Soon, Charlie and Evelyn spoke their goodbyes, and Jacqueline went to her bedroom. Gemma tried to stay longer to keep comforting Abigail, but Abigail refused, pleading how she only wanted a good night's sleep. So, with much reluctance, Gemma left.

She kicked off her slippers and laid across the bed. Where had the gentlemen taken themselves off to? She rolled over to face the windows and thought over the many twists and turns the evening had taken. Each thought returned to Barrett and his determination to make Uncle Theo see reason.

Gemma smiled, remembering his fierce determination. While most thought him a wicked bachelor who caroused, gambled, and drank, it had all been an act to hide his true intentions. Gemma hoped Uncle Theo changed his opinion of Barrett.

She drifted asleep with dreams of Barrett within her reach.

Sometime during the night, Gemma heard noises in the hallway. She jerked awake and rushed to the door, believing Barrett had come for her. She cracked the door open to usher him inside when she realized it was her cousin Lucas knocking on Abigail's door. He was whispering for Abigail to answer him, among other unintelligible words. In his slurred speech, he kept professing his apologies. The longer it took Abigail to open the door, the louder Lucas grew.

Abigail wouldn't open her door for Lucas. She thought she had to toe the line with propriety too strictly. She wouldn't give the servants any room for gossip.

Gemma took pity on them, opened the door wider, and walked over to Lucas. "Lucas, leave Abigail alone. Whatever you have to say can wait until the morning." Gemma laid her hand over his fist before he knocked again.

"Only want to explain," Lucas slurred.

"Tomorrow."

Gemma guided Lucas away toward his bedroom in the opposite wing. Lucas stumbled along, his mutterings growing louder. Part of her wanted to sympathize with him, but her loyalty lay with Abigail. She had watched her best friend pine over her cousin for years, grasping for any of his affection. When the season began and Lucas voiced his displeasure over Abigail enjoying the season, it had hurt Abigail something fierce. And for that, Gemma held displeasure with Lucas.

Her frustration had grown this evening when he hadn't shown any kind regard for Selina. He needed to get his priorities in order. Sooner instead of later. Until he did, Gemma would help Abigail and Selina cope as a friend would.

Before they reached Lucas's bedroom, he stumbled into a table and knocked over a vase. Gemma tried to keep him quiet so as not to wake anyone but failed. Duncan threw his door open and stalked out, ready to do battle. His vest and coat were thrown off and the cravat hung open around his neck. Gemma shrieked when he struck his hand forward and she saw a blade.

"Sorry, lass, I did not mean to frighten you." He lowered and slid the knife back into his boot. "It sounded as if we were under attack."

"No. Just a drunk Lucas trying to wake the household, or more like Abigail."

"Aye. I should have known he would have stopped by the lass's bedroom. Let me take him off your hands." Duncan relieved her hold on Lucas.

"Duncan, you must speak with him. He cannot bother Abigail any longer. Her heart will not take much more," Gemma pleaded.

Duncan nodded and helped Lucas into his bedroom. She wanted to say more to Duncan, but it wasn't the right moment. Lucas needed to be put to bed, and everyone needed time to let this evening's announcement settle in. Once the shock calmed, Gemma would help ease the stress any way she could. Since the gentlemen had returned, she needed to speak to Uncle Theo.

Gemma ran down the stairs to his study. The door stood open in welcome for any late-night visitors. Her uncle lounged in his favorite chair, smoking a cigar. When she stepped into his sight, he smiled and put the cigar out. "Take a seat, child."

Gemma tilted her head. "Were you expecting me?"

He laughed. "Yes. However, you took longer to appear than I thought."

She shut the door behind her. "There was a minor disturbance near my room that needed taken care of."

"Mmm. And did you take care of it?"

Gemma sat down. "For now, but I fear there might be more in the future."

Colebourne nodded. "Yes. I am afraid there will be too. But that is another issue I will deal with later. For now, we have your future to discuss."

Gemma straightened her back. "I will not wed Graham Worthington."

Colebourne raised an eyebrow. "You realize you have no say. I am your guardian, and if I chose him for a husband, then you will speak your vows to him."

Gemma scoffed. "Please. You must drop the stern, domineering act when we both know you are a soft teddy bear who will allow me to decide which gentleman I wish to marry. And I choose Lord Ralston."

Colebourne laughed. "You are getting right to the heart of the matter."

"What an excellent choice of words. Yes, I suppose I am. There are more than enough long, drawn-out dramatics with this family. I see no need to add to them. I know what I want."

"All right then."

Gemma sat forward in disbelief. "All right? You will not argue the point with me?"

Colebourne sighed. "There is no need."

"I do not understand."

Gemma had been ready to argue her points with her uncle. She had strong declarations on why Ralston was her soul mate. However, her uncle wasn't giving her a chance. He'd only accepted her decision with an "All right then."

Colebourne chuckled at his niece's dismay. Gemma had always been the one who bantered with him, even when she disagreed. He probably should have let her continue, but the events from this evening had worn him out.

Colebourne didn't want Gemma to suffer any doubts when, all along, Ralston had been the gentleman he chose for her. He only needed Ralston to get his affairs in order before he approved of the match. This evening proved Ralston was the gentleman for his romantic niece.

"What do you not understand? You love him and he loves you."

Gemma frowned. "Will you give him your permission when he calls?"

"I already have." Colebourne smirked.

Gemma blinked in surprise. "You have?"

Colebourne chuckled. "Yes, dear."

"Oh." Gemma sat confused. If Uncle Theo had given Ralston permission, then why hadn't he come after her?

"He promised to call on you tomorrow."

Gemma's brows drew together in confusion. "Why?"

"Why what?"

"Why did you announce I was to wed Worth?"

Colebourne rested his hands across his middle. "To gauge Ralston's reaction and see how honorable he is."

"But Ralston was not at dinner."

Colebourne chuckled. "Ah, but I knew he would appear."

Gemma narrowed her gaze. "How?"

"There were many principals in play that guaranteed his arrival."

"Principals you put into motion?"

Colebourne shrugged, a devious grin spreading across his face.

Gemma tilted her head. "And if he did not show?"

"Then he was not the gentleman for you, and Graham Worthington would be."

Gemma frowned. "That was not fair to trap Worth."

"Was it not? Mr. Worthington took it upon himself to help Lord Ralston with your ruination. Does a certain carriage ride come to mind? Or perhaps a few other instances when he helped to cover for his friend after he knew Ralston had ruined you," Colebourne reasoned.

A blush spread across Gemma's cheek. She opened her mouth to respond, but clamped it shut. How had Uncle Theo learned of those instances? She thought he was clueless about her stolen moments with Ralston. There was nothing to say that wouldn't implicate her. Many times she'd stretched the truth when trying to cover for her little misdemeanors in life, but she never lied to her uncle and she wouldn't start now.

"I am sorry for shaming you."

"Ahh, Gemma. I feel no shame for you, only extreme pride. You followed your heart and 'tis all I have ever wanted for you."

Gemma winced. "Even though it was scandalous?"

Colebourne winked. "That is what made it even more exciting to watch."

"You are wicked, Uncle Theo." Gemma laughed.

Colebourne waggled his eyebrows. "I think the correct term is mad, my dear."

Gemma giggled. "Oh, you are definitely that too."

"I knew Ralston was the gentleman for you when I invited him to the house party."

Gemma wrinkled her nose. "Then why forbid him to pursue me?"

"To place that yearning within each of your reaches and to see if your love for one another held strong enough to grasp. Ralston became smitten at the first sight of you. However, I was not ready for him to pursue you during the house party, so I threatened him away."

"Why?"

Colebourne sat forward in his chair and reached for Gemma's hand. "Because I wanted you to enjoy the season. You had waited for so long with romantic notions about finding a gentleman who would romance you through the season. I watched your attention on Ralston throughout the house party and knew he was the one for you when you wouldn't pay attention to any other gentleman. Once we arrived in London, I dangled my forbiddance of him, knowing you couldn't resist Ralston and the temptations he offered you."

"Sneaky. What would have happened had someone caught us?"

Colebourne shrugged. "Then we would have weathered the scandal as Holbrookes do."

"Very risky."

"Yes, but worth it for your happiness. I never had to worry over you, as I have your cousins. While they had a difficult time adjusting after the accident, you never did. I know you suffered their loss, but you never lost your sense of who you were. You kept your positive approach to life and dreamed of romantic love. I wanted you to experience the thrill of falling in love. Have you?"

Gemma sighed. "Yes."

"Perfect. Now off to bed with you, for your Romeo shall call tomorrow, bright and early."

Colebourne rose and helped Gemma rise. Gemma jumped up and wrapped Uncle Theo in a tight hug. With his matchmaking madness, he had made it possible for Gemma to have an adventure in romance. While highly improper, it only proved to her how much her uncle loved her.

"I love you, Uncle Theo."

"Love you too, missy."

Gemma skipped to the door, happy to know Barrett would come for her soon. Perhaps he even waited for her in her bedroom now.

"Oh, and Gemma?"

She turned. "Yes?"

"I have taken precautions to secure the secret passageways tonight. No one can enter or leave them."

Gemma blushed. "You knew?"

His eyes twinkled. "There is nothing I do not know that happens in the walls of my home."

Gemma placed her hands on her hips. "Then you are aware of Abigail's suffering?"

Colebourne nodded. "Yes, and all will be well soon for Abigail. For now, let us focus on your happy nuptials. I am sure Ralston will waste no time in gaining a special license."

"You cannot allow Lucas and Selina to wed," Gemma ordered.

"Gemma, they are none of your concern. Lucas and Selina will wed. Now good night." Colebourne sat behind his desk.

"Good night, Uncle Theo."

Gemma left with a disheartened look. While she'd found happiness in her own forthcoming union with Lord Ralston, she still wanted to protect her family from unhappiness. She thought he would force an unwanted marriage on his son.

However, it was far from what he wished to do. He wished the same as Gemma. He wanted Lucas to find happiness with his soul mate and his only true love. But it wasn't Colebourne's life to take control of. He could give gentle nudges, but it was up to the parties involved to stake their own claims.

"They will both wed. But hopefully to other souls."

Chapter Twenty

After Ralston had disrupted their dinner the evening before, the gentlemen discussed Worth and his business venture. His father declared his approval at his newfound focus in life, and Colebourne gave Worth and him the evidence they needed to secure Lady Langdale's arrest. However, when they went to capture her, she had already disappeared. With Colebourne's support, the authorities allowed them to stay on the case and sought their assistance with other open cases. It gave their business a sense of security they lacked. After a few drinks, Worth forgave him and congratulated him on winning the lady's hand.

Now Ralston waited in his carriage for the last hour, watching Colebourne's house. Over the course of the hour, he'd had his servants deliver gifts to Gemma every ten minutes. He chuckled when, after the last delivery of flowers arrived, Gemma followed the servant out onto the steps. Her gaze searched up and down the street for any sign of him. She was a vision to watch.

She stood on the steps wearing a soft pink confection, her hair decorated in the red ribbons from the first gift he gave her. The color reminded him of cherries, which reminded him of her sweet lips. Lips her teeth were dragging across while she looked for him. He wondered if she wore the sweet scent of vanilla he'd sent for a second gift. Her chaperone, Lady Forrester, came to the door and ushered Gemma back inside.

Ralston chuckled and decided not to make her wait any longer. He patted his chest, confirming the box still rested in his inside pocket. He'd prepared a grand gesture to ask her to marry him after the duke gave his permission.

He strolled up the sidewalk, eager to ask Gemma to be his wife. Before he could knock on the door, it flew open and Gemma jumped into his arms. She wrapped her arms around his neck and pulled his head down for a kiss. He tried to resist, but as soon as her lips connected with his, he lost himself in the pleasure of her greeting. He didn't know if it was only a few seconds or minutes before a throat cleared, interrupting them. Gemma tasted like heaven.

Ralston pulled his lips away with agonizing slowness to see the Duke of Colebourne with his arms crossed, standing next to Lady Forrester. If it weren't for the twinkle in the old man's eyes, his scowl would have frightened Ralston. It was a front he'd discovered last night once he learned of the duke's softness toward Gemma.

Ralston nodded. "Your Grace."

Colebourne arched a brow. "Lord Ralston, I see you have finally decided to grace us with your presence."

"I intended to woo Gemma with romantic gestures."

He chuckled. "We noticed. However, you only caused a whirlwind of impatience to descend upon our household."

"My answer is yes," Gemma said with excitement.

"Uhm …"

Colebourne laughed. "Let the poor bloke ask the question first."

Gemma beamed. "Oh. But he does not need to."

"But I think he might want to," whispered Colebourne. "Good luck, my boy, you are going to need it with this one." Colebourne slapped Ralston on the back as he walked away from them.

"Gemma, please wait in the parlor while I welcome our guest," ordered Lady Forrester.

Gemma untangled her arms around Ralston, but not before brushing a kiss across his cheek. She sauntered away, stopping at the door and looking over her shoulder at him. Gone was the gaze of an innocent lady eager for a marriage proposal. A sultry siren replaced her, sending him a stare filled with scandal and seduction. Ralston gulped, undone by the simple change of her gaze.

"Lord Ralston?"

Ralston heard his name in the fog of his desires. Desires awakened by the simplest of kisses. His focus lost by her touch. His intentions forgotten by the message in her look.

A throat cleared again. "Lord Ralston?"

Ralston turned his head slowly toward Lady Forrester, his eyes still focused on Gemma. "Yes, Lady Forrester."

Lady Forrester cackled with glee. "I love when a match comes together."

"Excuse me?"

"Nothing, young man. I can only allow you a short time alone with Gemma before I must interrupt."

He nodded, his focus still on Gemma.

Lady Forrester motioned for him to follow Gemma. "I suggest you make the most of your time."

The realization of Lady Forrester's gesture sent Ralston into motion. The words *alone* and *Gemma* were the only ones he wanted to hear. He strode toward his intended, wrapped his arms around her, and twirled her inside the parlor. He closed the door and pressed Gemma against it. She slowly slid along his body, and he captured her lips under his.

His kiss spoke of his every desire. Gemma's mouth opened under his, and his tongue slid inside, ravishing her with his demands. Each pull of her lips under his drove him insane. He couldn't get enough of her, needed her underneath him. Ralston wanted to plunge into her depths until they both screamed their love for the universe to hear.

His desires came to a halt when he heard giggling on the other side of the door. Then the lady in his arms broke out in laughter.

"They are listening," whispered Gemma.

"Who?" he whispered in return.

"My family."

"Oh?"

Gemma smirked. "Yes. I am afraid it is a nasty habit we all have."

"Eavesdropping?"

"Yes."

Ralston grinned wickedly. "Then allow me to entertain them."

"How?"

Ralston dropped his arms from around her and knelt on the ground on one knee in front of her. Her gasp told him his gesture pleased her. He pulled out the box from his coat and opened it, offering it to Gemma.

"Gemma, love of my life. I have been most scandalous in my courtship to win your heart. However, kneeling before you now, I only want to act the proper gentleman and declare the love I hold for you shall always rule my heart. Even with improper acts, they will always be with the utmost devotion. I love you more than the day before. Will you honor me with your hand in marriage? I promise to hold it in mine forever."

Tears streamed down Gemma's cheeks. Ralston would have been alarmed had it not been for the smile lighting her face. Gemma had nodded throughout his entire speech and kept nodding now. Her hand grasped his, holding tight. Ralston slipped the ring on her finger and drew her down to him. He wiped away her tears with his knuckle. With a gentle kiss, he drew out her answer on his lips. A breathy "Yes." escaped with the gentle caress.

He lifted his head and stared into her eyes. "Yes?" he whispered.

"Yes. Yes. Yes." Each answer was whispered with a kiss.

Ralston sighed. "Yes."

"I love you, Barrett. I promise to keep your hand clutched in mine forever."

Ralston rose and drew Gemma to her feet. He led them to the settee. Sitting down, he drew her in his lap. Their time alone was limited, and he wanted her as close as possible.

She swatted him on the shoulder. "Why did you make me wait all day?"

He grinned. "I wanted for you to experience the romantic gestures of a courtship. Even though it is only a short courtship. Because I do not plan on waiting for a long engagement."

"Your presents were very sweet. So, I forgive you. But I am afraid Uncle Theo will insist on a wedding."

"But I have a special license."

Lady Forrester spoke inside the room. "One that will do you no good. Gemma will have a proper wedding. I have already discussed this with your mother."

Ralston sighed, knowing they outnumbered him. Lady Forrester didn't give him enough time alone with Gemma. However, he would have a lifetime filled with her by his side. Gemma smiled at him, and he knew he would never forgive himself if he didn't give her a proper wedding.

"Your wedding may be proper, but I promise your wedding night shall be full of scandalous surprises," Ralston whispered in Gemma's ear before the rest of her family descended on them.

Epilogue

Ralston backed Gemma toward the bed with much impatience. She was finally his, and he wanted to draw her soul into his. Her fingers tugged on his buttons with her own impatience. They had agreed to the demands from their families and waited the proper three weeks after the church read the banns. His mother wanted them to marry at the family's estate, and Gemma had agreed to accommodate his mother. She had bonded with his parents and sisters while they planned the wedding.

However, now he couldn't wait any longer to make her his again. The strict attention of a chaperone had kept them apart all these weeks. They had watched over Gemma more during their engagement than before he'd asked for her hand.

"Can I tear this gown from your body? I do not think I can wait much longer," Ralston growled.

She gave him a chiding glance. "No, you cannot. It was my mother's gown and our daughter will wear it one day."

"Daughter? I like the sound of that. But before the special occasion can come to light, we must remove this monstrosity. Turn, and I mean quickly."

Gemma's husky laughter sent a fierce reaction to his cock. If he was hard before, every touch, kiss, and sound from Gemma only strengthened his desire. His fingers made swift work of the buttons. He realized there were only five main buttons to undo, and the rest were decoration. Ralston peeled the garment from Gemma. Before long, she stood naked before him. He placed a kiss on her shoulder, his hand circling around to cup her breast. Gemma shuddered when his finger pinched her nipple.

Ralston closed his eyes, drawing in a deep breath to slow down. He'd promised Gemma a wedding night full of scandalous acts. If he didn't get himself under control, the evening would be over before it even began.

Gemma turned in his arms, her face lit with her siren smile, and started to undress him. "Your turn."

Ralston wanted to rip his clothes from his body, but there was determination in his wife's gaze and the pleasure she gave him with her kisses and soft caresses was too good to refuse. Soon he stood naked, ready for their night of decadence delight. He laid her on the bed and lowered himself over her.

"I must have you now. I promise to love you more leisurely after I fulfill this need."

"Promise?"

Ralston nodded. His body shook with need.

Gemma wrapped her arms around his neck and her legs around his waist, opening herself wide. "Then, Lord Ralston, you must take me now with much haste. Because if you do not, then I fear I shall perish without your love from the ache that is consuming me."

"Then, Lady Ralston, let me relieve your yearnings."

Ralston took Gemma, forging the promise they made today to love one another forever. Over and over throughout the night, they secured the promise they made to one another. Lord Ralston lived up to his promise to love Gemma slowly, and Lady Ralston lived up to her promise to love Barrett with the same passion.

In the early morning dawn, with the cool air brushing across their bodies, they lay staring into each other's eyes.

"Do you imagine we created a daughter to wear your wedding gown?" Ralston teased.

Gemma smiled impishly. "No need to imagine when we have already accomplished the act."

Ralston's eyes grew wide as he stared at the sweet smile lighting Gemma's face. She reached for his hand and placed it across her stomach. Ralston tenderly caressed her, and a silly grin covered his face. Without a doubt, Gemma had always known Ralston was the man for her, and he'd never given her any reason to believe otherwise. Even now, his gentleness humbled her. Her rake of a husband held the character of a true gentleman. One that would make a fine husband and even grander father.

Ralston couldn't believe his luck in life. Not only had he found the woman of his dreams, but now she was his wife. Even more amazing was the gift she was giving him. If anyone would have ever told him he would fall in love at first sight, he would have called them all kinds of a fool. However, he was the fool who fell hard for a tempting siren with a luring smile.

"I love you, Gemma, and will love this little rascal we created with all my heart forever."

"I love you, Barrett. And our child is not a rascal but a sweet angel."

"We shall see." Ralston chuckled, drawing Gemma into his arms to love her all over again.

~~~

Read Selina & Duncan's story in

How the Scot Stole the Bride

~~~

If you would like to hear my latest news then visit my website www.lauraabarnes.com to join my mailing list.

~~~

"Thank you for reading How the Rake Tempted the Lady. Gaining exposure as an independent author relies mostly on word-of-mouth, so if you have the time and inclination, please consider leaving a short review wherever you can."

~~~

If you love the Matchmaking Madness series then you'll love my new spin-off series Fate of the Worthingtons. The series involves Reese Worthington's siblings as they find their soul mates. It involves some suspenseful mystery as they attempt to capture the elusive Lady Langdale. Uncle Theo makes a few appearances along with some other characters from the Matchmaking Madness series. Check out the first book in the series today.

The Tempting Minx (Fate of the Worthingtons #1)

Desire other books to read by Laura A. Barnes

Enjoy these other historical romances:

Fate of the Worthingtons Series
The Tempting Minx

The Seductive Temptress

The Fiery Vixen

The Siren's Gentleman

~~~~~

Matchmaking Madness Series:
How the Lady Charmed the Marquess

How the Earl Fell for His Countess

How the Rake Tempted the Lady

How the Scot Stole the Bride

How the Lady Seduced the Viscount

How the Lord Married His Lady

~~~~~

Tricking the Scoundrels Series:
Whom Shall I Kiss... An Earl, A Marquess, or A Duke?

Whom Shall I Marry... An Earl or A Duke?

I Shall Love the Earl

The Scoundrel's Wager

The Forgiven Scoundrel

~~~~~

Author Laura A. Barnes

International selling author Laura A. Barnes fell in love with writing in the second grade. After her first creative writing assignment, she knew what she wanted to become. Many years went by with Laura filling her head full of story ideas and some funny fish songs she wrote while fishing with her family. Thirty-seven years later, she made her dreams a reality. With her debut novel *Rescued By the Captain*, she has set out on the path she always dreamed about.

When not writing, Laura can be found devouring her favorite romance books. Laura is married to her own Prince Charming (who for some reason or another thinks the heroes in her books are about him) and they have three wonderful children and two sweet grandbabies. Besides her love of reading and writing, Laura loves to travel. With her passport stamped in England, Scotland, and Ireland; she hopes to add more countries to her list soon.

While Laura isn't very good on the social media front, she loves to hear from her readers. You can find her on the following platforms:

You can visit her at *www.lauraabarnes.com* to join her mailing list.

Website: **http://www.lauraabarnes.com**

Amazon: **https://amazon.com/author/lauraabarnes**

Goodreads: https://www.goodreads.com/author/show/16332844.Laura_A_Barnes

Facebook: **https://www.facebook.com/AuthorLauraA.Barnes/**

Instagram: **https://www.instagram.com/labarnesauthor/**

Twitter: **https://twitter.com/labarnesauthor**

TikTok: **https://www.tiktok.com/@labarnesauthor**

BookBub: **https://www.bookbub.com/profile/laura-a-barnes**

Manufactured by Amazon.ca
Bolton, ON

31869428R00141